The Tyrant Under the Skin

Caroline Sanders

Copyright © 2014 Caroline Sanders
Revised Edition Copyright © 2025 Caroline Sanders
All rights reserved
ISBN: 9798306669694

Dedication

This book is dedicated to those who are struggling against tyranny

Acknowledgements

To Mum and Dad, for inspiring me with their passion and principles. To all my family and friends for their support and love.

To Sol and Ivo, for the magic and the joy they bring, for their compassion and their fearless originality.

To Rob, for his eccentric creativity, insight, and love: without whom I could make nothing real.

Contents

Prologue 1
Chapter 1 3
Chapter 2 7
Chapter 3 12
Chapter 4 17
Chapter 5 23
Chapter 6 28
Chapter 7 32
Chapter 8 39
Chapter 9 47
Chapter 10 55
Chapter 11 60
Chapter 12 65
Chapter 13 69
Chapter 14 74
Chapter 15 79
Chapter 16 83
Chapter 17 86
Chapter 18 90
Chapter 19 97

Chapter 20	102
Chapter 21	106
Chapter 22	111
Chapter 23	117
Chapter 24	122
Epilogue	127
Notes	129
Appendix 1	133
Appendix 2	139

Prologue

Cogito ergo sum.*

The grass bends in breeze that wisps clouds above. She strokes my cheek and steals my breath for her own. Is this true? The immediate truth of sensation is clear and yet could still be hallucination, could still be an illusion of a trickster God. However, I don't believe in God and so I trust my sensation, for now. My story is strange however, and hides behind corners and in shadows, languidly slipping away like the horsetails above my head. I can't touch it and it's not certain, not clear. It is a fiction, and yet within must be truth, existential truths that have been experienced, as well as some facts that are actual historical events. History is only ever constructed, part fiction and part truth. The best story will win, or the perspective of those that hold power will win.

I shall tell you one story about this time. A story about what can happen when you live on an ocean, swept along by waves of fortune. A story told from the perspective of someone who has no power, and resists power. Is there another way to live your life, a determined, fated way? In a small way this is a moral tale of the contingent and the necessary, and warns us of what happens when people forget their contingency and become as necessary to themselves as gravity is to the planet; the fascists' journey. Fairy tales scare our children with howling wolves and cackling witches, but wiser counsel suggests vigilance towards the tyrant stamping his feet within us, and the tyrant marching blackly outside.

This story's concern is six months in a century that questions what we can know, beginning with the dualism of Descartes and ending with the empiricism of Locke. It's a time that gives voice to fascism, liberalism and anarchism. It's a time of establishing the certain in a time of uncertainty. It is May 1649 in England and the King is dead …

Part One

*A man must make his opportunity, as oft as find it.**

Chapter 1

Brilliana Barebone was eighteen when she decided that her mother's advice was wrong, and confirmed to herself that she would take the left-hand path to market. The path concerned was overgrown with yellow-darted grasses and fur-tongued nettles. These curses pricked at her conscience when they needled her legs and ankles, compelling her dance towards the black cauldron of trees on the hill. She didn't want to disobey, but it was quicker to walk through the trees, and she was not scared. Swaddled within Prospero's Grove, as a baby and child, she had believed in silver unicorns and fiery dragons, but these had long since melted into air. Today was not for childish conceits as she had a more important worldly task ahead of her. She heard the cattle groan helplessly as she passed them, convulsive with milk, whilst high in the clouds the yellow wagtails composed a hopeful mood for her with their songs. The May Queen enchanted her with summer's ornaments on that day, but Brilliana was not so easily distracted.

Within fifteen minutes Brilliana was wrapped up in the bustle and stench of the town, and the trees had disappeared behind the smoking coughs of the stallholder fires. She pushed through the damp, fat smeared clothing of the hurly burly crowd to the sugar loaf shop. The white bullets glistened with sweet hope and Brilliana licked her lips, as she had a sweet tooth. 'A pennyworth please,' she asked.

Without noticing the gloom, she blinked at the shopkeeper, who was a large man swaddled in sticky sweat like a rich caramel sauce. He carved a slice from the sugar cone and passed it reluctantly to his customer. He was resentful at each sale; possessive of the produce he sold. The blue paper clutched at the sugar and Brilliana tucked it swiftly into the pocket at her hip, before sliding stickily out of the shop.

Northampton Castle lay to the southwest of the market and Brilliana's house lay to the east. Northampton was a walled town and was still famed for the livestock markets held there. Sheep, cows and horses wandered petulantly through the town, trying to ignore their master's switch, and this added to the confusion and damp sweat that perfumed the air and lagged the throat. Since Cromwell, a rival trade had usurped in notoriety however, for the town now made the shoes for the New Model Army. The parliamentarian character had seeped into the cobbles and the thatches of the architecture. Men worked

CHAPTER 1

tirelessly for the democratic ideal where God was held in purity, without gem or ornament. The talk was simple but impassioned and the Sabbath was kept steadfastly. It was a sincere place to live, but it irked Brilliana who sensed there should be more to an ideal than the modest diligence of service.

She slid out of the shop into a pensive air. A scraggy man with startled hair and a brown snakeskin face leaned over to grin. 'You should get home. The Levellers are coming, astride their mutinous fire-horses, Cromwell behind, bearing thunder and lightning. It is blessed revenge from God. It will be the end!' The man chuckled.

Brilliana suffocated by the smug foreboding hustled herself away towards the castle side of town. She knew of the Levellers. The last few years had been a time of dreams and visions of the future. The market had been full of men shouting against the King, shouting for Parliament. Ideas had collided and been sacrificed in a firework display of thought. Cromwell had won and the King was dead. They had all fought with him, fearlessly, for ideas and for dreams. He was their protector, had brought them closer to God. The Bible itself was the word of God, not the King or the Bishops. Political power must be consistent with this religious certainty. Northampton men served Cromwell and served God. Service and sacrifice.

The monarchy was formerly abolished on the 6th of February 1649 and Parliament stated in a public decree that, "The office of the king in this nation is unnecessary, burdensome and dangerous to the liberty, society and public interest of the people."*

Cromwell was made Chairman of the Council of State. He was also head of a formidable army: an army more radical than Cromwell himself, an army infiltrated by radical Levellers who demanded more pay. Harder to satisfy for Cromwell was their demand for the extension of the franchise: for every male head of house to be able to vote for members of Parliament, regardless of property ownership. The Puritan Cromwell, saturated with original sin, was tormented in his dreams by dread demons of anarchy, made free in the land when every man had political power. Political power held without the conservative constraint of self-interested property ownership. These men would have nothing to lose. This was not the word of God; this was the word of the Devil.

The political debates had ended in 1647, and yet she knew that these more radical ideas still smouldered, still bubbled steam to be inhaled. The Levellers and Freeborn John produced some smoke. Brilliana felt a flutter of excitement at the sound of the pirate Levellers coming to town. She smoothed down her tangled brown hair, and moistened her pale orchid lips, as if preparing for a dance. Like a dryad used to hiding shyly in shadowed groves, she dressed herself for the glamour of this new world and the battle ahead. She hoped she could use her enchantments as armour.

Chapter 2

That afternoon Brilliana lay stiffly on her hostile bed, staring idly at the mottled, brown ceiling above her. The mottles transfigured into shapes, the shapes into faces. She saw the scared face of her mother, dry and brittle, patched with worry and fear. The mother faded into grandmother, firmer and wider in her features, more open and broad. Brilliana smiled at the memory of her grandmother smuggling sweet bread and stories. Of course, she was not really her grandmother at all, but a great aunt who had looked after her mother when her own mother had died. That was a story that had puzzled and scared Brilliana in the twilight of childhood.

The Northampton Witch Trials thirty years earlier had been a sensation, before even the Pendle Witch Trials. The six witches were tried in Northampton Castle during Lent Assizes. It was the first time that water ordeal had been used as a judge of supernaturalism. Three had gone through water ordeal and three had been hanged at Abington Gallows. The charges were bewitchment of people, cattle, and pigs. The witches had allegedly cursed and caused death to overcome at least one poor soul. One woman had been accused of bewitching a smock so that it became covered in frogs, toads and other ugly creatures, which frightened the local children. It made Brilliana tremble as she imagined what her grandmother had felt before she tumbled into the freezing water that had unapologetically flooded into her mouth, throat and lungs. She had drowned. There was no witchcraft, except the witchcraft that leaves a child without a mother. It was this story, whispered to her by her great aunt on foggy nights, where she had first heard the phrase, 'authority turned to tyranny', uttered by one of the witches before their death. This phrase was the witches' legacy.

Her mother interrupted her thoughts, 'Brilliana, come and help, you lazy girl.' She tumbled softly off the bed and slunk down to the kitchen. She plunged hands into flour and felt the soft welcome of the dough. Her mother was talking to Brilliana's older brother. 'William it's not right, you can't go with those men. They're bad. Stay out of it please. Levellers cause trouble wherever they are. Cromwell will put them down, and you with them. We need you to earn us money. Stop your fanciful ways'.

'What's going on?' asked Brilliana. Brilliana's mother looked sternly at her daughter, 'There are Levellers coming Brilliana and town will be ablaze with trouble before nightfall. William is dancing with the Devil, and his

Chapter 2

idleness will get him troubled.' She looked wearily at her eldest son.

Katherine Barebone was a careworn woman. She had some kind of idealism born of her mother and aunt, but she was also rotten with fear and cowardice. Her values were eaten through by a life spent in tacit avoidance, and, haunted by her own mother, she wove a tight web around her children. She assembled vague superstitions and paranoia, which she slung like garments over her small frame. She feared neighbours and friends and pushed the external world away from her as if it were a plate of poisoned fish. She rarely went out, and wished her children would do the same. Sometimes at night she would wake screaming in terror, feeling a black shadow pressing down on her chest. It would take her husband hours to calm her. They both feared the Devil was breathing in the same night air as they. Both were religious: the religion of vengeful curses, of fire and brimstone, of guilt and trial, of sin on Earth. Yet, despite these infections that burrowed into her spirit, like worms into an apple, there were still the remnants of idealist thought, of belief in something better, an idea that she was wronged and that her mother was wronged. But it was the fear that people were bad, the Devil was at work, and that Earth was dammed because of it, which had won her. Heaven was her ideal, and it was only there that judgement could be true, could be final and perfect. She feared life and longed for death.

William was frightening her, she felt a cold chill creep down her spine as she listened to his desire. Her head throbbed and her gaze blackened, William's words faded into a dull rush of steam circling through her ears and clouding her eyes. She slumped forward onto the wooden table.

Brilliana and William lifted her small scant body that had resisted the world for over forty years. It was light and airy, full of the holes of fear and cowardice, like a bone eaten by infection. Her breath was small and shallow as they lay her on the bed and covered her. They were not infected by fear and worry, however, and had seen their mother like this many times. Brilliana caught the gaze of William's gooseberry green eyes and smiled. They raced down the stairs. 'What have you heard?' Brilliana blustered the words in bullets.

'The Levellers are coming. The New Model Army has mutinied and they are riding here, to Northampton, to raise a Leveller army. Cromwell is over. He is a tyrant, like the King. They are to demand equality,' William smiled. 'I'm going to join them Brilliana. I'm packing now to head to town.'

'What do they demand?' Brilliana stretched her mind to Heaven.

'Equality, Brilliana.' He grabbed her arm, 'All men to have a say in laws, to have a say in who runs our world, and I'm for that. Not just the Lord of Abington Manor, to vote, but our own father, and every man with house and home.'

William raced around the kitchen fetching bread and clothes, holding them to him like totems. Brilliana tossed the witch's phrase, 'authority turned to tyranny,' around like driftwood on waves gasping at the world around her,

CHAPTER 2

crashing down on the bits of her life that beached that idea. It felt like her heart, her soul, was spoken in that phrase. The words were the fear that her mother had retreated from, but for her it was a truth to be learnt and used to change the world around her. Brilliana and William's first good fortune was a sickly mother and a hardworking, God-fearing father. This had meant carefree and careless time alone or nurtured by their heretic great-aunt and had allowed them to develop imagination and a free spirit. Although they had no formal education, their family did use rich religious vocabulary and an invisible hand linked the brother and sister to their distinct family history.

William lurched a kiss at her forehead and ran like a hare loose from a trap, out of the door and into the sun. He turned, his face haloed, 'Come with me?' Brilliana smiled, and shook her head, content for William to change the world. Her place was here, and she waved him goodbye.

Chapter 3

Brilliana stirred the black pot hanging like a pendulum over the fire. Her excitement at William's departure felt tortured now as she heard the heavy, reluctant step of her father on the doorstep. He shadowed into the house, gloomy and stern as always. The pendulum pot ticked away the approach of dinner as the shadow solidified into leaden presence at the table. Brilliana muttered that mother was resting upstairs and that William had gone, her eyes fixed on the table in hopeful distance.

Inside the kitchen the firelight danced shadows onto the surfaces and John Barebone watched these shadows closely as he listened to Brilliana's words. He felt angry at the day. He had worked as hard as always, but his master had been scathing of his ideas on farming, ideas that John had volunteered during a rare break in work. These ideas were sorely gained from years of labouring experience. In fact his master had loudly humiliated him in front of the other labourers. The other labourers had seized on this ridicule like vultures on a rotting carcass, and had spent the rest of the day laughing at him, and pretending to bow and scrape, mocking his vain pretension. They hated John for years of showing them up by working harder and refusing breaks. The blamed him for eroding their quality of working life, for creating an unreasonable expectation in their master about working conditions. It was bad enough that enclosures had begun in the Midlands, with the loss of personal farming land that it had entailed, but to be working for a master harder than they had ever worked for themselves was criminal. They had enjoyed a rare chance to humiliate this man.

John was profoundly resentful that his master had treated him so badly, and was deeply humiliated by the other labourers. The news that William had left home, without discussing it with him was further insult. He was deeply shamed and this one certain truth reflected at him in the light and shadow theatre before him, and within the eyes of his daughter looking sullenly at the table.

He began to pray with eyes fixed shut, blocking out a world that he believed to be a trick of a Devil. Everything was placed to tempt, to test him, and he could see the twist of demon tail, of demon smile within every object. He believed nothing that his senses told him; it was all illusion and trickery. He had slowly disconnected his mind from his body over the years, like a rider dismounting a horse. This horse was sulphuric in colour and smell. The smell of sulphur infected his nose, and his eyes filled with sharp tears. He had heard her say that his son had left home. He had heard her say that his pathetic wife was useless again. She was a work of the Devil, that daughter. He moaned at the cursed life, the tricks, the suffering that this sulphuric devil conjured for him.

In that instant, he finally wrenched his mind from his body, and dismounted that sulphuric horse. Like Abraham before him, he heard the treacle voice of an Angel deep within the fog of his mind. He had waited for this all of his life: the word of God, finally talking to him, rewarding him, choosing him. In his elation John heard an Angel tell him that the world was not real, his daughter standing before him was a demon, the food she stirred was filth from Hell itself, and none of this disgusting depravity was anything to do with the godly John Barebone. John Barebone, after all, saw through this trickery, he was too clever and too pure to fall for Lucifer's torments. 'To release the horse is to release the devil. Let it run,' whispered the Angel. 'It is God's will, it must be.'

Brilliana felt a black pain spread sharp through her shoulders as she hit the cold stone floor. She was stamped on, hard-heeled into the stone, and as time stuttered and space shrank, a crouching incubus pinned her to the floor. As she twisted, she saw the small grimy eyes of her father, closed and wet, his lips bridled and drawn back. He bit into her face. Her mercurial mind surged into her body to resist and attack. The struggle was timeless, empty, and cold. His fist punched her stomach like an icy sunburst and she wrapped around his fist like a breath, before pulling the pain back into her lungs to force his legs, his fist away.

CHAPTER 3

They fell, locked together into deep, black, well water, conjured from another place. It filled her ears and eyes as she tangled in the green weed that wrapped tightly around her wrists and ankles, making escape impossible. The water gushed down her throat, saturating and dissipating her breath. As she opened her eyes she saw her father's horse-face grinding his teeth before her in clairvoyant vision of Fuseli's Nightmare. He could not swim and he had lost control. The fear bubbled out of his mouth, forming rainbow spheres; orbs of light that gathered around her like fairy fish and floated her up to the surface.

She was still without thought, her mind still liquid throughout her body as she ran from her father. John Barebone was weak, like his wife. The doubt that questioned the reality of the world around also stripped away his physical strength. His puritanical Christianity, by denying the body had led John into harm. He had delighted in injuring himself in his work, as evidence of his purity. Each blow his body took was a blow against the duplicity of demons, evidence of his ability to see through the trickery. The pain of his body was the pain of Jesus. John was a farm labourer and he would work harder than anyone. He would refuse any comfort, any break, as proof of his godliness. He would take the most difficult tasks, the most dangerous tasks and would enjoy the pain. In the end his old body, after times of starvation and hard days labouring in the fields, lacked the strength to finally overcome his daughter, and she escaped.

The first words that returned to her were the words, 'William,' and 'Levellers.' These words reverberated like notes in a symphony, referring to other notes and other words, returning meaning to her world, returning an idea of herself to her. She would find William and join him and the Levellers in Northampton. She smelt the air alight with the fragrance of May blossom and felt the wet grass stroke her legs in tearful agreement.

Chapter 4

The day Nathaniel Elkin had heard of the death of the King had been a day of portent and foreboding: January the 30th, 1649, four months earlier. That day the clouds had gloomily gathered and glumly hung close to ground for the day of execution. The earth lay brittle and cold as the world snapped. Women miscarried in bleeding shock, animals moaned in dank fear and the men worked grimly and silently, lips and hearts pursed.

Nathaniel swept the grey-grained floor of The Lord's Arms, near Kirby Hall, hands wearily frostbitten and eyes blurred by dust. Tall and thin, his beer-black hair swung in limp curls around his ears. Grey, fish-fin eyes sparkled at the world around him, but it was impossible to see the depth in them. The battle at Naseby a few years earlier had lost Nathaniel his father and brother, both loyal to Cromwell and both sacrificed to the victory. He felt the loss as a bleary, dull ache in his head, in the background of any experience, smudging any joy. He lacked the language to make sense of any physical or emotional sensation and so felt it all to be cold and brutal. He hovered apart from the world around. Nathaniel was an intelligent man though he did not possess an extensive vocabulary. He had no formal education and his family practiced silence as daily meditation.

Mr Chappell had employed him at the inn because of his fine mathematical mind. His father had understood and valued mathematical language and had taught this to Nathaniel and his brother, which had led to this good fortune in employment. This gave Nathaniel the opportunity to listen closely to the words used in the conversations at the Inn, and he was developing the language to explain a subtler apprehension of the world to himself with every day that passed.

The men had gathered at tables to discuss in urgent voices the ill portended news. This is it. Cromwell and God will protect us. The vanity of the King is vanquished, we are on the true path to God.' A small, petty, rat of a man, named Elber Choke, chimed with the news and traced a river of ale on the worn table. He had fought out of impoverished necessity and wrapped in fear he had fated himself to Cromwell and felt the lottery was his. He quoted the clichéd words practiced that morning on the rat-run to the inn. His allegiance to one king and to then to another was smoothly insignificant, being less to do with noble ideal than with calculated egoism. He was more surprised than anyone at the victory and the execution of the King. He wasn't used to winning, but had intuited that the world

CHAPTER 4

was changing, an intuition developed by a life of desperation at the edge of survival. For once the harvest was bountiful, and he had arrived at the inn cloaked in self-satisfaction.

Thomas Shobbe, a local landowner, coughed in wholehearted agreement. 'My fear is that without a king, we descend into anarchy. Cromwell must gain power and quell that danger. He is a strong man, the fearsome fighter we know as the Ironside. The strongest must rule, might is right! These people,' he waved nonchalantly in the direction of Elber Choke and other imaginary miscreants, 'are robbers and murderers, they need a strong hand. I care not for Cromwell's view of God, but I care that I'm not robbed or murdered in my bed.'

'You have a dim view of humanity, Thomas.' A pale, quiet man spoke, shaking a shock of curly brown hair with piercing blue eyes. 'I think that man, without tyranny of monarchy, will be released into rational consideration of good government.'

Thomas coughed again in studied irritation, but Elber Choke had lost interest in the discussion and was staring at an old man standing behind the bar. The ebony man was tall and slim, dressed in fine, neat clothes, with greying curly hair. His black skin gleamed in the sharp, winter sunlight that danced through the open window at the side of the Inn. Choke scurried to Nathaniel and hurried him outside. Nathaniel explained that the old man was James Chappell, who by all accounts had been the first black landlord in England, and quite famous for it years ago. He had saved his master, Sir Christopher Hatton, and Hatton's family from a fire at Kirby Hall and had been richly rewarded in Hatton's will. Choke rang his hands in anxiety, and his hair stood up, fearfully alarmed, in escape from his own shrewish face.

He hustled himself back to the table where the voices were shuddering in anger. 'You are young; you don't know people, like I do. I know what people are like. Shallow murderers who would sell their own grandmother for a penny, we must fight for Cromwell and for control.' Thomas was an old man of fifty some years, hefty in build, ruddy faced and with little tolerance for drink or people. He had known the Leveller, John Sedgewood for many years and he despised him. He stood up and wavered for a moment, his face red with the imagined fear and swung a coarse fist towards the Leveller. Within seconds tables were overturned, jugs spilling slimy rivers and waterfalls on the grainy wood, and the two men knotted into a torment of each other.

Choke scurried off, without turning his head, bound for London. The black man at the bar disturbed his vision. It was not that he hadn't seen black men before; after all it was his business to see them, to weigh them up, and to judge them for his employer in London. It was rather that the picture of a black man in charge of his own destiny was deeply troubling to him. He rubbed his eyes as if to rub the man out, as if he was a mistaken line in a drawing, an error to be erased. He was scared, uneasy, and it blurred his sight and gnawed his stomach. The world had turned upside down. He knew the old King and the new one, Cromwell, would continue the slave trade, but these

CHAPTER 4

Levellers, and the True Levellers, they wanted everything to change. He comforted himself that even if the days of profiting from the black African slaves were ending, the Irish indentured servants and labourers were becoming more plentiful, and could even become foremost in transport to Montserrat. Choke got more profit from the indentured labourers because he mostly sourced them himself from the prisons, and from the streets, using debt entrapments of bread and beer. The numbers of poor had swelled after enclosures, famines and Cromwell's war on the Irish Catholic population. Sometimes Choke paid families for their grown up children if he could be sure of a return. Some even wanted to escape to the Americas, not knowing the conditions they would find themselves in once there.

Nathaniel returned wearily to his home that evening. His mother was crafting dinner out of cabbage, her hair dripping into the pot. They didn't speak and he slumped in the hard wooden chair by the impotent fire. The world felt hard-bitten to him, steely and unforgiving. He watched his mother with absent-minded focus, as she swiped the musty children away from her work. The King was dead, and everything had changed, abstracted Nathaniel. He realised that he was untouched by the death; it had altered nothing for him. He levitated above the mood like a ghost, mourning his own life rather than the death of the King. He envied the men at the inn with their anger and their feeling. He felt nothing except the hard edges around him, which bruised the soul beneath his skin. His mother grumbled incoherently at him. Tace Elkin was not given to idle speech. It was time to leave, thought Nathaniel, time to find a softer surface to pour onto.

The next morning was brisk and frosty. He clattered the pennies from the rest of his wages onto the table, gathered a few belongings and set out for the town. The hard-edged environment in which he had grown up had stunted his moral character. He was unforgiving in his escape and left his mother and siblings without means to survive. The pennies would last a week at most. It was a selfish act, by a man not given to selfishness, but a man without developed virtue or vice. Nathaniel had not become any kind of man, good nor bad. He was acting in the moment, without hesitation and doubt as he lacked the voice to express these to himself. Nevertheless he was certainly making a choice. It was the choice of a child who says, 'No!'

Chapter 5

Nathaniel felt the gnawing hunger clutch at his stomach as he trudged tirelessly towards the spire in the distance. He had slept a cold, irritated sleep under a bare oak the night before but could now see the town in the distance and felt his legs move in eagerness towards the future. This bodily eagerness was not matched by his thoughts, which were slow and cautious being dominated by physical desire only.

Within hours he heard the excited rattle of voices, and smelt the sweet fragrance of woodsmoke, before he noticed the sour undercurrent of livestock stench that lingered in the air. He decided to find food. Nathaniel slumped under a tired wooden window, pulled a glum rag from his pocket, placing it on the dusty earth, waiting for the pennies to fall. Puritanism, although believing that poverty was a spiritual opportunity, also understood that there was a duty to help those in desperate need, and so

Nathaniel was hopeful. As dusk gripped the throat of the town, Nathaniel slurped a thin, peppered broth, smiling quietly at his success.

Days passed and he toured the steaming town for the best places to beg. The best places were decided by a careful calculation of comfort; soft and sheltered from the wind and rain, for the winter was a wet and cold one, against density of passing traffic. However, a more subtle calculation revealed to him that times of the day and days of the week were variable factors, and Nathaniel's childlike mind was kept easily occupied.

The sun was gently warming Nathaniel one frost-brittle morning when a small goat-like woman curled up beside him in the doorway. 'Are you ok, me duck? Mind if I join you?' She butted her way into the space using a bony elbow as a lever. Wedging herself down she appeared lost in the coloured rags that stuck around her like a grimy whirlpool. Her upturned face shone like milk in the sunshine, as she smiled at Nathaniel.

'Had much luck me duck? I've been begging this town for as long as I can remember and it's a right old stingy place. Hate it, going to leave soon, for Oxford or London, some big place where I'll get a chance. Only came here for a wedding party, never went back to me home. Horrible wedding too, nasty people, hope they're dead! Going to make my money and then go off to a better place than this. You know I'm engaged to a rich man, worldly you know. He'll be waiting for me return I bet. Not going back to him though, he'd beat a lamb that took too long to roast that

Chapter 5

one, no going back to him. For me it's a fine life in a big town, not this rat hole.'

'Why are you here then?' He asked. She had leached into his mind and was drawing out his innate curiosity. 'To get money of course, then pay to get to a big town. Nearly got enough when I was bleedin' robbed by those Edison crooks, think they own these doorways they do, but they don't, not even the King does anymore,' and she let out a peel of throaty laughter. 'It's all planned me duck, not long now and I'll be gone to something better.'

Nathaniel was caught in the whirlpool surrounding this woman, a whirlpool of rags and grime excused by ambition and dream. He had never really thought about his future, his thoughts only describing the present to him in basic terms of hunger and need. He had no plans, although his body appeared to move towards something. Of course that could simply be the category of time acting upon him, fooling him into the future, and giving the illusion of will. Rebellion was as far as he had got in his existential development. He had arrived in Northampton because he had left his home when it had become something unpleasant to him. It was hard and he had longed for something soft.

The woman's words troubled him and he felt as if he was standing on the edge of a cliff, wanting to jump. He wanted to plan and to think of a future, but feared it more than anything else in the world. This possibility that he could jump, that nothing was stopping him, filled him with anxiety and dread. Had he nurtured a secret hope for happiness whilst sitting by his mothers fire? Is that why he was here? If so, he had hidden it well, even from himself. He felt he would fall into an abyss filled with black-eyed monsters.

The two companions sat wedged in the doorway like driftwood beached on a cruel stone unable to move, whilst coins bounced on the rag like dull chimes measuring out the day in pity. Nathaniel started thinking about tomorrow; he started dreaming and so missed the clue that something was wrong. He heard a shrewish scream from next to him, and then awoke on a cold floor that chilled the fiery ache of his body.

Confusion clamped his mind as he stumbled in the dark. He heard a squeak and scurry, but could see nothing. He called out into an echo and heard sombre voices masked by madness in reply. Fear hammered a violent rhythm deep within his chest and his fingers slid on the damp, slimy stone that broke his chaotic fall. Although Nathaniel had only thoughts of a child, he was not stupid. He simply lacked the language to explain the adult world, to explain moral life, and to explain creative life. He paused from his chaotic staggering and remembered a phrase from the inn a few days ago. 'Hurry ye to the debtors prison.' He was in a prison, he was certain of it. Begging was illegal and the punishment was certain imprisonment. He sat amongst the rats and the filth and sobbed, a single, dry, desperate sob, the third one of his life.

It was impossible to say how much time had passed. There was no day and night, just gloom. Sometimes a torch lit the green stained walls and a bowl was shoved through a small opening in the door. It tasted of nothing but

Chapter 5

emptiness. Nathaniel could see nothing and hear little. Deprived of his senses he retreated once more into the unexplored inner world. It was not rich, but inhabited by odd phrases learnt from the inn and shallow memories. He remembered the words of rebellion, and they seemed like tiny fires scattered in a wasteland, like he had seen once after Naseby where his father and brother had died. He pictured his mother again. His mind and his heart were mostly unfeeling, for he didn't have the words to explain subtle sensitivity, but like a child crying for milk, he felt sadness at his lack of emotional nourishment, and cried out for his mother.

Empty of sensation and of meaningful thought and memory, Nathanial's mind travelled to a familiar place of certainty. He had felt each damp brick in his cell and counted each one. He measured the edges of each brick with his thumb, and calculated the area and perimeters, and tried to calculate the area of his cell. This place of numbers was solid and beautiful. Nathanial knew this language, for he had always been good with numbers, he felt at home with them. He began to create number patterns and lost in the complexity he felt a contentment creep into his heart. Sometimes he felt angered when his concentration became dulled by a voice in the distance, but he would begin again without hesitation and with a deeper and more profound conviction. Mathematical language described the fabric of the universe to Nathaniel, and in a sense life itself; the language of God, of certainty, of objectivity, and for three months it saved Nathaniel's life.

Chapter 6

Brilliana caught her brother in a tight embrace. She had run like a cat, jumping off upturned logs and over streams on the path to Northampton. She hung tight to his neck, and he swung round in surprise. 'You changed your mind?'

Brilliana didn't want to describe the events that had led her to that choice, so she just screamed out in excited agreement. William scratched in his bag for a piece of rough bread which he held out for his sister. She grinned and bit into the sandpaper like dough in gratitude. From their high vantage point in the north-east, they could see the town spread out before them, looking like a stony beach, with sea foam snaking between the pebbles. They felt like giants. The smoke that wisped around the houses created a magical veil around and above the town. Brilliana grinned at William, her cheeks bulging.

Chapter 6

Brilliana and William shared the look of autumn between them. Their hair shone like newly opened conkers, run though with wisps of gold and their eyes both watered in green and brown pools, the colour of leaves in September. William, however, was taller than Brilliana, and his hair was rough and short, much like his manner and his conversation could be sometimes. Brilliana's hair was long and sometimes knotted, and she was more languid and complex in manner than her brother.

Several hours later they felt the heat and dirt of the town. The feeling of excitement was tangible, as young and old bustled around the market square and the Drapery, not shopping, but waiting in a busy frenetic way. 'They'll be here any time now,' explained a pompous, stout old man, to a gathering crowd of anticipators. 'The horses are blowing in from the west, from Banbury, they are running scared from Cromwell and from God.'

The man felt his role in events was to explain the facts to the simple folk before him. He enjoyed imparting information because it made him feel important. He relished the opportunity to appear impartial and objective, as this also made him seem an expert on these current events.

'I hope they bring food,' muttered a short man to the left of Brilliana, and the gathered crowd around nodded their agreement. Poverty was rife in Northampton and food prices were high. Wheat prices had reached ten shillings a bushel. 'The Levellers will give us land,' shouted a young man, 'we need common land to grow some food. Those enclosures of the land, started here in Northamptonshire, have ruined us and made our children hungry!'

The older man twitched in alarm and shouted out to calm the crowd. 'Fear not good folks, we landowners will help you as soon as these Levellers have been put down by Cromwell. The answer is not in Leveller thieving, for that is not God's will and your souls would fear on Judgement Day, but in waiting for the crops, and labouring hard on that land until harvest. You will be paid fair.'

'But paid fair makes no difference with prices so high and no way to sustain ourselves by independent means. Why am I waiting for your mercy and good will?' The young man was walking menacingly. A ripple of applause followed him. 'Shall we riot again?' Laughed another man in the crowd. Forty years before, in 1607, and remembered by a few in the crowd, there had been riots in Northamptonshire against the arch-Catholic Tresham family, who had enclosed the common land. Captain Pouch had led those riots, promising to protect protestors by the contents of his pouch. In fact his pouch had only contained some green cheese, but nonetheless there had been several months of rioting and it had passed into folklore. The people of Northampton were not scared to take action. They had been against Catholicism since that day and sang easily and fervently in support of the Protestant Cromwell as a consequence.

The mood was broken by the sound of shouts and horses from the castle in the south. As if one body the crowd started running towards the noise, transmuting the menace into excitement. The Landowner jumped from his

CHAPTER 6

perch and waddled away from the noise like a pheasant from a gun. Brilliana and William clutched at each other and let the crowd push them along.

Chapter 7

The battle horses of the Levellers snorted with anger, on behalf of their masters, as they galloped towards Northampton. The sea-horse memories of white foam dampened their black leather bridles, whilst steam dripped out of their volcanic nostrils. The men were wrapped in hot sweat and cold wind, which shivered them to the bone. They were heading to the castle for refuge from the wrath that bit hard at their ankles. Mutineers were killed without a second thought in Cromwell's army. These men were half dead already, for only men with nothing to lose would have considered so dangerous an action as mutiny. They were half dead from starvation and from exhaustion. Thompson demanded more pay and a vote. They just wanted more food. They all agreed that the death of the King had brought no sincere change in their circumstance and Thompson had become their only hope. Any change, even death, was better than stasis.

CHAPTER 7

Life was trampled thoughtlessly beneath them as they fixed their sight on the brown sludge of river that circled the castle walls. The square panoptical keep rose authoritatively behind, unwelcoming but safe. The castle was easily overwhelmed as it had little protection, wrapped soft in Godly complacency as it was.

Sir Arthur Haselrig owned Northampton Castle but had leased it out to various individuals who had set up ramshackle houses in the trenches. He was rarely there and the castle had a life of its own as a collection of individuals and families engaged in commercial activity, rather than as a protected fortress. The castle was Norman with extensive grounds and was surrounded by deep trenches and earth bulwarks. The knight himself was one of the five members of Parliament whom King Charles I tried to arrest in 1642, an event which led to the start of the English Civil War. He fought beside Cromwell and was in Scotland with him in 1649.

The Levellers ransacked the wood-wormed rooms stuffing golden coins into their pigskin pouches. Captain William Thompson sat astride a battle black horse, exhausted from mutiny and war. He was not exceptional in appearance; his will and energy were saved for his mind, which was indeed exceptional. Seventy men and horses stretched around him; all that was left after the mutiny at Banbury and the battles with Cromwell's men. His brother had fled to Burford with the others and Thompson missed and feared for him. All that mattered now was the message of equality and freedom that had cost him so much. It mattered because it had to matter,

Thompson felt sure it had cost him his life: "Farewell hope, and with hope farewell fear."* John Milton thought these words earlier that year, words that he would publish some twenty years later, but Thompson was living them in the moments since the Banbury mutiny.

Captain William Thompson had been a great soldier, not because of his strength and courage but because of his strategic mind. He was a plotter and a conspirator. He enjoyed the game, the battle of wills, more than the battle of swords. He had been instrumental in planning key victories for the New Model Army in the long fight against the King. He was at his best when he plotted with conviction. Cromwell had won his mind with his anti-royalist rhetoric, but Thompson, like all intuitively clever people, soon felt the corrupted ideal like a boil that needed lancing.

Cromwell, like emperors before him, had caught light with democratic fervour, but this idealism was too strong for him and had burnt a terrible shadow into his ego as it took him over. He was deluded that the fire was his own. Ideas start fires, transmuting dull and weak characters into bright beacons for a short time until they burn out. Cromwell was not the Platonic philosopher-king, but a soldier. He was not able to control the fire or understand what it was, but he mistakenly loved it as power derived from his own charisma. He told himself that God determined his destiny and his certainty. He was fated to be the Lord Protector. It was right because God had chosen him. To others he justified his grip on power in the same way as Augustus had, by arguing that the people were not ready for political decision making, that they would make bad decisions, they would starve without a father in charge, they were barbarians and England would descend into anarchy. He had to assume power to save England. It was his Duty, and derived from God. He was a necessary truth for England and for God.

Thompson used his strategic mind to plan his next attack. It was to be a purely political attack and in the heart of Cromwell country. This attack was for the mind of the Puritan town that had made the boots and shoes for his army, without which Cromwell would surely have lost the war. If he could win the Leveller message in Northampton, then whether or not he or his brother survived, perhaps the idea would live.

The Leveller men knew what to do. They gathered their warhorses into the town, their bridles garbed with sea-green ribbons. Swirls of people gathered and pressed around them, currents of unease and dissatisfaction. Grabbing the large brown pouches swinging from their saddles, the Levellers conjured shining gold coins from them like they were seaside magicians. The crowd, silenced in awe, were beached onto curious houses that pressed hard into the ebb and flow of the people below. There was a breath that was still and waiting and then the pirates flung the coins out into the crowd. The people erupted in spasms as if a muscle that had been cramped. They burst the banks of the houses and spilt out into the alleys and courtyards. The wealth of the castle was spread through the town like a glorious yellow river, as if the sun itself had been captured, it's light shining into every heart present in that small market town. The Levellers shouted to the people that this gold should be the people's gold, that it had been stolen by the landowners when they stole their land for the enclosures and had thrown them off the land like vermin. The crowd cheered.

The next thing that happened was even more astonishing to Brilliana. The Levellers had reached the market square. Pushing past the pigs and sheep Thompson rode to the perch where the landowner had been speaking an hour before. He leaned forward and the crowd fell silent:

"The faith of the Parliament and the Army has been broken by the treachery of some prominent people. Petitioners for common freedom have been suppressed by force and petitioners abused and terrified. Bloody and tyrannical courts have been erected, the civil laws have stopped and been subverted, and the military introduced to torment and vex the people. All of the lives, liberties, and estates have been subdued to the wills of these tyrannical men in power; no law, no justice, no right or freedom, no ease of grievances, no removal of unjust barbarous taxes, no regard to the cries and groans of the poor to be had, whilst utter beggary and famine has swept through our nation.

We are therefore forced to defend and preserve ourselves and our natural rights, and to set the unjustly imprisoned free, to relieve the poor, and settle this Common-wealth upon the grounds of Common Right, Freedom, and Safety.

Be it therefore known to all the free People of England, and to the whole world, that, (choosing rather to die for Freedom than to live as slaves) we have gathered and associated together with our swords in our hands, to redeem our selves from slavery and oppression, to avenge the blood of War shed in the time of Peace. We declare from the integrity of our hearts that by the help and might of God we will endeavour the absolute settlement of this distracted Nation, upon that form and method by way of an Agreement of the People."*

As Thompson made his impassioned speech to the shining, gilded crowd, a trail of dirty, manacled men were led before him and their iron chains were clumsily, and brutally broken. These men were a sad show compared to the Leveller pirates. Most were in prison for beggary, which was a crime; humiliated to begging after being thrown off their subsistence land. Confused and bleary from days and months spent in darkness, some sank scared to the ground, rocking on their knees, swallowed up by their rags. Others looked around, feeling the promise of the words settle on their hearts like butterflies. These particular men ran to the edges of the crowd, covering themselves in that camouflage. Thompson declared the prisoners of Northampton freemen, unjustly imprisoned by a tyrannical power disguised as democracy. 'Authority turned to tyranny' he said, and Brilliana's heart fluttered.

The Levellers moved through the crowd like great ships ploughing a deep, heavy sea. They handed out the stolen gold, white pamphlets entitled, An Agreement of the People, and sea-green ribbons. William pinned the ribbon and clutched a pamphlet to him tenderly. Although he couldn't read, Thompson's words had lit a fire and he wanted an ember to carry, to blow upon, to keep alight.

Over the mottled heads he saw Captain Thompson high on his horse, shouting to his men. He couldn't hear the words but the Levellers were cheering, the people were cheering and Captain Thompson was saluting the crowd. Northampton could be a Leveller town.

Chapter 8

Nathaniel swept his lank, black hair out of his eyes. He was bewildered. The last hour had been a confusion of rough voices in the dark, being pulled and pushed out of the labyrinth of tunnels and cells under the castle, and squinting through daylight. He had hidden in the hard-edged crowd but the crowd were mumbling slowly away and he felt uneasy. Nathaniel's stomach griped at his mind. He was ravenous.

A leathery man with startled grey hair stood patiently beside Nathaniel. Curiosity had led him to the Market Square but he was disappointed by the show and was nauseated at the words that Thompson had spoken. He felt like a doctor diagnosing a sickly disease and fearing the contagion. However he felt sure this disease was weak and he knew that Cromwell's men were charging, at God's speed, to Northampton and would cure this plague with fire and brimstone. He smirked at the Leveller words to banish them. His arrogance seemed to stretch him taller as he noticed the prisoners being released. The release of prisoners interested Elber Choke greatly and went some way to curing his nausea. He saw some of the prisoners run swiftly into the crowd and get consumed, but he cleverly caught one. This one stood beside him now, tall and strong. Choke knew that he could get a good price for this one at the docks. He was young and could have a long productive life ahead of him in the Americas. He reminded Choke of some of the indentured Irish labourers he had recently sent to the slave masters in Montserrat. Cromwell, and King Charles before him, had taken Irish men, women and children for indentured servitude in the Caribbean. They had been thrown off their lands, forced into debt and often charged with treason. Choke was sure that as long as Cromwell remained in charge, this would continue and he would be employed. He smiled happily at his fortune.

'Would you like something to eat young man?' Nathaniel twisted his head towards the short man standing beside him. The man smiled easily at Nathaniel and Nathaniel dropped to his knees to avoid the bending and twisting that hurt his back and his neck. Choke opened a large bag held at his side and fetched out bread and a small piece of cheese that disappeared in seconds. Nathaniel closed his eyes and drank some warm beer and sat still on the ground.

The crowd had mostly dispersed as it was heading towards evening and the Levellers had long gone, back to the castle it was assumed. The crowd were anxious

CHAPTER 8

though, they knew Cromwell's men would be on their way and they wanted to shelter away from the forthcoming battle. Choke was also anxious. He knew he had to leave with this man before the army arrived, to ensure their safety and his money. It was an investment after the bread, cheese and beer payment.

'So you were in prison', he spoke softly whilst playing with the remainder of the bread. 'You should be careful, you know, Cromwell's men are on their way and if they catch you here they will surely put you back in your cell, or worse?' Choke continued to absent-mindedly play with the food, like a cat playing with a mouse. 'Have you family here?'

Nathaniel sat still with his eyes closed, trying to remember his mother, but his mind was dark and fogged by fear. He shook his head. 'Come with me then and I'll find us a safe place'. Nathaniel, half starved and fearful, nodded quietly and started to stand up. Apprehension trickled down his skin like warm butter. He had met this man before, he thought, back at the inn. He tried to remember him, but his mind was enfeebled and his fear was much stronger. Choke grabbed his arm; his fingers carving into his skin and muscle as if to print himself onto Nathaniel like a branding. He pushed Nathaniel though the flotsam, holding onto him tightly. A few men shouted, drunk and impassioned, whilst the women sat laughing in groups, and children ran in rings through the damp emotion left by the Leveller army.

Behind a clutch of children, Brilliana and William sat waiting for the next act. They bristled with excitement, eyes wide. William, alight with ideas of freedom and justice, felt omnipotent. He had waited for this moment for years. He was a true Leveller and knew with absolute certainty that he would follow Thompson to the stars in the Heavens. He wanted to fight. He silently called Cromwell's men to hurry, his exaltation was to die for freedom rather than live as a slave.

The pinch on Nathaniel's arm cut hard into his skin. The pain was sharp and he felt it deep in his head where it woke his slumbering mind. He remembered this man. It was the slaver who had been to the inn a couple of times, before catching sight of the landlord, Mr Chappell. Nathaniel remembered him scurrying away like the rat he was, and Mr Chappell saying that he would have thrown him out anyway and that a Slaver was a disgusting job, the very worst. He saw the disgust on Mr Chappell's face like a visible stain. Mr Chappell had given Nathaniel a job, and had praised his counting skills and Nathaniel thought he was a good man.

Nathaniel mind wandered lazily as hunger again clouded his focus. He had been honest when he left his mother, he thought. He had left money so that she could buy food for the family, which was kind. Nonetheless a niggling doubt gnawed at him and his mind wondered how his mother was getting on without him. Sure, a mouth less to feed, but a wage less for all that. This was the first time that Nathaniel had thought or questioned his own actions. He decided that he had been honest, but he had not been kind. He was not sure that Mr. Chappell would have thought he was good.

CHAPTER 8

The pinch on his arm burnt his skin, finally awakening him to the realisation that he was in desperate danger from this slaver. Choke was gripping his arm like a man grips a rabbit caught in a trap moments before he's beaten the breath from its body. Fear twitched at his nerves, pulling his arm away from the tight snatch of Choke's fingers. His arm stretched out and pulled hotly at his elbow and shoulder. Choke span around to look at Nathaniel. 'His fiery warhorses are on their way to send you to eternal damnation if they find you!' He spat 'You're mine now. You ate my bread and my cheese, and you drank my beer. You have no money to pay me. You are a debtor. You are my debtor. And you should thank our God that you are mine because I am your only hope to escape certain torture and death from Cromwell's men. And yes they will torture, they will push hot spikes into your skin until you plead for death. And after death, you will spend eternity in the pits of fiery Hell for your crimes against God. An Eternity, do you hear me. This is God's will, ' Elber Choke spat these words into Nathaniel's ear, 'unless you do penance with me now.'

Nathaniel snapped at skin with kicking knees, but he was weak in both body and mind, and Choke's words were like weevils weakening his will and eating through his resolve. He fell back onto his knees, hot tears scarring his face. He felt himself being dragged through the dirt.

William interrogated closely the scene of the two men scuffling in front of him. The smaller snake-skinned man seemed to be spitting at the other, who looked taller and stronger, but was dirty and thin as a rope. Brilliana looked up too from the picture she was drawing in the dirt; a sketch of the horse that Thompson had been riding. She was quite pleased, as she had exaggerated the head and nostrils to make it seem fiercer than it had actually looked. She wanted William to look at it and looked up to catch his eye. She had always wanted William's good opinion of her, but he always seemed out of reach, looking into the future and away from her and their life, and although he was kind to her, it was hard to get his attention. William was indeed looking intently at the struggling men and Brilliana knew hers was a lost cause. She brushed her shoes over the picture and followed Williams gaze.

'That man scared me when I came for the sugar,' she muttered, nodding towards Elber Choke. The men had stopped struggling and the smaller one appeared to be dragging the other like a rag though the dirt. William felt the fire rush through his chest. The snakeskin man was dragging the other like he was not human, like a man would drag an object, without dignity or care. Men were not objects, but had thoughts and feeling, had desires about their futures, made choices about themselves and their actions. If Thompson's words meant anything, they meant that William had to act against this injustice and to act for freedom. He ran towards the two men, elevated by righteousness and broke Choke's grip with one punch to his leathery skin.

Nathaniel lay crumpled on the ground as William and Brilliana stood blinking at him. The rat man scurried into the evening mist after the first punch. Choke was not a stupid man and had lived by his wits for many years. This self-interested egoist quickly weighed up the situation, and decided to save himself. It was over in an easy breath, and left William elated as the ease reassured his righteousness.

'You grab his head, and I'll grab his feet,' ordered William. They carried him gently over to a shop doorway where they arranged him as comfortably as they could. William had food and drink in his satchel and they shared it between them, but their bodies were leaden with exhaustion and so they ate without words. The sun sank thankfully, like an expectant mother into her bed, and the companions drifted into their own stuttering sleep. Nathaniel was briefly aware of a soft surface in the lap beside him, and he poured himself onto it gratefully. Brilliana smoothed Nathaniel's hair hopelessly fighting her vertigo to sleep, and William slept like a Leveller, wrapped in courage and conviction.

Elber Choke lifted the tankard to his thin, bitter lips. He simmered to himself, determined to get back what was his. He owned that man. Cromwell would be here tomorrow. Those Levellers would be dead. 'Might is right,' he thought and raised his tankard. 'It's God's will.'

Part Two

*Hell is empty and all the devils are here.**

Chapter 9

The sun rose and hid gloomily behind grey clouds the next day, as though worried at what he would bring by his presence. Brilliana woke first and William soon after. They were hungry, cold and tired. Nathaniel's eyes blinked with confusion, his head lying softly in the cauldron of Brilliana's lap. 'Who are you?' He asked.

'I am William Barebone, and this is my sister Brilliana Barebone. We have come to fight with the Levellers for equality and justice against the tyrant Cromwell'. William sounded pompous, thought Brilliana, but she smiled at him, remembering the same tone in his voice when he had been instructed to look after her as a child.

'Nathaniel Elkin' whispered Nathaniel as he staggered to his feet. They had slept beside a large cornhusk of a door, and the stone porch had breathed patiently for them, softening its edges in dewy pools. The three friends explained themselves to each other in hushed and grateful tones whilst they adjusted their earth pocked clothes. Brilliana ran her fingers through her hair but was met by knots and tangles that would have frightened a sheep shearer. She smoothed it down instead and turned her green flickering eyes to her brother. Sinking lazily back down onto the porch, she settled her back to the door resigned to an hour or more of William and Nathanial staking their claims and defining their boundaries to each other.

Brilliana spoke with a honeyed tone, sugary because of the demands of her sweet tooth. She did not talk much, however, and thought most people were overbearing in conversation. She included her brother in this, but it didn't stop her loving him as she had decided long ago that this was a feature of human beings and human interaction and just couldn't be helped. She, however, was more interested in losing herself, as this desperate clutch onto self seemed to cause pain and suffering. She had no strong sense of self, and wasn't convinced that there really was an eternal, unchanging self, which is perhaps why people clung on to their ideas of themselves so desperately in company. Brilliana enjoyed experience and any sense of self came only through experience. She knew she existed because she felt the sun on her neck. She knew that the sun was hot because she burnt herself red raw in the sunshine. She was rooted in the world, rebelling against parents who had rejected the world as the illusion of a demon. She felt a pain in her stomach as it lurched in sudden unwelcomed remembrance of her father. She breathed slowly and let

CHAPTER 9

the feeling go, separating from the pain and fear as thin shadows from the past, lacking the intensity and variety of present sensation.

The cornhusk of a door bristled open and Brilliana fell into the hole, legs high in the air. Cow-brown eyes gazed down at her, and a halo of hay-smoked hair shimmered around the smiling face. 'What have we here then?'

Brilliana staggered to her feet sweeping the shame away with restless movements of her hands down her skirts. Her thoughts were bumbled and she knew she was just staring. William and Nathaniel stood close by, silent in apprehension.

Margaret Prince was in her early fifties with hair greying and face wrinkling, despite her youthful heart. She looked at the three tired expectant faces and knew they were refugees with common purpose, as she spotted the sea-green ribbons attached to William and Brilliana's clothes. She smiled a wide smile and bustled them into a small, grey kitchen with a kettled fire and darkened chairs. The three friends slunk down and sipped at wooden bowls hastily pushed into their cold hands. They explained themselves again and told of their Leveller allegiance as Margaret busied herself around their flotsam. She washed pot after pot and swept the grey flagstone floor, listening with a wry smile playing around her lips. Then she sat down, gathered up her seaweed knitting and began to talk,

'My son is Thomas Prince. He is a Leveller and is imprisoned in London as we speak. Imprisoned for criticising Cromwell. That great Cromwell who was going to save us from royalty, was going to spread democracy, equality, liberty and justice in our land. We fought for him, at his side. We lost friends, brothers, fathers, mothers for honest and sincere ideals, but we believed in him, we all did. Oh joyful day when we won and the Puritan drum beat set the Earth's heartbeat. Thomas and his Leveller friends, John Lilburne, Richard Overton, and William Walwyn, thought it was just the beginning. Overthrowing the King was a first step on the road to true equality and justice. But Cromwell got drunk on power, not used to intoxicants, he could not resist the temptation.' She shook her head and pursed her thin lips in disappointment. 'He told Thomas that the people weren't ready, that they need a leader to tell them what to do, but Thomas could hear the drunken slur in his voice as he described his blurred vision of a tyrannical future and a king without a crown.

William felt a crackle rise along his backbone, as if it were a lightning rod caught fire by the electricity in her words. Each vertebrae smouldered and he stretched his back high to reach the clouds above, as if each cloud would open to reveal riches for him.

'We Levellers have to be heard and understood. We want political equality and justice, not anarchy. We want a Parliament that is consented to by all the people, voted for by all the people, and laws that are made by them that protect the liberty of all people, not just the rich landowners. We're not anarchists, we know there will be economic rich and poor, some will have more and some will have less, that is determined by the needs of liberty and freedom herself. We must be free to own and produce what we determine for ourselves. But economic inequality

CHAPTER 9

should not determine distribution of justice and liberty. Political equality protects equal distribution of liberty and justice. All should be treated equally. Equal justice, equal liberty, and equal political freedoms.'

She was fierce and impassioned, like Minerva herself. She had lost her good husband to fever fifteen years ago, on the cow-poxed, rain soaked fields of Yorkshire. The loss was spectral, haunting her every moment. Sometimes she felt lost to insanity, but her son rescued her, with his words, his passion and his politics. She was a wealthy woman, the daughter of gentry with the privilege that contingency bestowed. Her own father had looked after her and her son, until Thomas had left for the Civil War. He had been imprisoned in March and Margaret had moved south to be nearer her son, and to press for his release.

'But what about women?' Brilliana muttered, as the ideas poured down onto her like rain. This woman was astonishing to her, utterly different from her wood-wormed mother, she gestured strength and independence and Brilliana absorbed her words like a sponge.

Margaret's mouth pursed. She had been lost in the familiar and the young voice dragged her back. 'We stand with our men, of course, their liberty is our liberty'. Margaret turned away, but she felt wretched suddenly. Margaret knew that there was no political place for women in a new democracy, not yet. Religion infested the political, expressing itself in Puritanism, and religion did not favour women. She grabbed at compromise and proudly presented a document, a petition written by Leveller women dated September the 11th 1648, which she read out to the three friends,

"Showeth that since we are assured of our creation in the image of God and of an interest in Christ equal unto men, as also for a proportional share in the freedoms of this Commonwealth, we cannot but wonder and grieve that we should appear so despicable in your eyes, as to be thought unworthy to petition or represent our grievances to this honourable house.

Nor will we ever rest until we have prevailed, that we, our husbands, friends, and servants, may not be liable to be abused, violated, and butchered at men's wills and pleasures. But if nothing will satisfy but the blood of those just men, those constant undaunted asserters of the peoples freedoms will satisfy your thirst, drink also, and be glutted with our blood, and let us all fall together: Take the blood of one more, and take all: slay one, slay all.

Nor shall we be satisfied, however you deal with our friends, except you free them from under their present extra-judicial imprisonment and force upon them, and give them full reparations for their forcible attachment.

Our houses being worse than prisons to us, and our lives worse than death, the sight of our husbands and children, matter of grief and sorrow and affliction to us, until you grant our desires, and therefore, if ever you intend any good to this miserable nation, harden not your hearts against petitions, nor deny us in things so evidently just and reasonable, as you would not be dishonourable to all posterity."*

Chapter 9

'This was signed by 10,000 Leveller women,' she added proudly. 'This is women's political voice today, presented in a petition to Parliament. We demand to fight and die for our beliefs; we demand the release of our husbands and sons. Perhaps one day we will have political equality, little one, but in the meantime you must fight for what is right.'

Margaret grimaced as she said these words, lucidly remembering a scene from three weeks earlier. A short, stout woman wearing a paprika red dress had been paraded down the Drapery to the market. She wore a grim-grey helmet and a mask polished with cruelty. It was a scolding bridal and she wore it as punishment for 'riotous speech'. The corruption of the court was overwhelming, and the judge listened for no more that thirty seconds before pronouncing sentence. Her husband laughed carelessly with his comrades, buoyant in the humiliating parade to the market place. She stood for an hour, anonymous and defaced, before she was collected by her husband, and bundled shamefully away like a parcel of old, stinking meat.

William interrupted her thoughts and asked whether they could stay until Cromwell's troops arrived, as they wanted to fight on the Levellers' side and defend the town from Cromwell. Margaret was glad of the company as she missed her son. She had nobody to talk with anymore after spending much of her life in the company of gentrified kin or with the fierce political soldiers that surrounded her son. Without a husband it was difficult for her to meet new companions in Northampton and retain decency, and the company of women mistrusted her. Her new friends spent the rest of the day laughing, talking and resting. She was delighted at the young Levellers and made soft warm beds for them to sleep easily on that evening.

Chapter 10

William Thompson drummed his coarse fingers on the even coarser table, and shouted angrily into the fireplace. The Levellers were in the large castle keep where they had liberated the prisoners and gold. It had not been hard to overcome the castle defences for Haselrig had not been worried about invasion, having believed the battles to be won. His men were with him in Scotland and Thompson was glad of the respite their absence afforded him. He worried for his brother and friends who had split away from them and gathered horses towards Burford in Oxfordshire. 'How long, Captain Thompson?' He heard the desperation in the voice that broke into his nocturnal thoughts, and replied in determined tone, 'today or tomorrow at most, before they are on us'.

The men were pensive as they waited for Cromwell's faithful to arrive. The soldiers were a mixed bunch of men; some were mercenaries whilst some had been conscripted at the start of the war. They shared dissent, a contagion that spreads when people live and work together, and share common lives. The masters of men, whose paternal aim is only to quarantine and cure, have long since seen dissent as a disease. They spend months, years and epochs thinking of strategies to divide men from each other to reduce the corruption. This infection, like most infections, is a disease of poverty and it spread easily amongst malnourished men. Curing the poverty would have been a more effective strategy than trying to quarantine the dissent.

Most had fought throughout the Civil War and were lucky to survive. It had been a hellish torture; the dizzy pain of hunger had tormented them on the edge of starvation for they earned the same pittance as an agricultural labourer. Many men had died from scurvy; skin smoked yellow with cavernous mouths and bulbous, bulging eyes. Typhoid also called souls to her and in their confusion and pain they could not escape. Some of the men had suffered wounds in battle. The flesh rotted on their bones and was cut away until, in some cases, the bone was laid bare. Some died in the intolerable stench, but some survived. There seemed no moral sense to this, but few questioned God's judgement.

The soldiers' feet were rubbed black, and became calloused like stone, unable to feel anymore. The shoes were not made for right or left feet, but one shoe was produced to fit both. Their Venice red uniforms scratched them until their skin matched in colour. The cold was deadening to all sense in winter, and tales were told of

Chapter 10

men taking days to thaw after their flesh had turned to crisp ice.

Mostly the life was boring, stultifying. Thoughts dried coarse like butterflies, caught dead in their minds. This tedium was, however, the best they could hope for. The worst was the suffering and the utter, soul-cleaving terror of battle. The fear of losing their minds during days of demonic pain where they would sound the cursed scream for Death was ever-present in their fragile minds.

William needed to be honest and sincere with them, as he, and all England owed them after Cromwell's betrayal. He must set himself apart from the enemy, because integrity was now all that he possessed. 'We must plan the battle. We have muskets and swords, some leather armour. Our horses are tired and worn, and some of us are on foot. We must use the castle defences as our own, for they will provide the only advantage we will have. Move the men to the trenches and bulwarks. We are not defending the castle simply using it, and we must ride out on my command if we are not defeating them. We will head northeast, as they will attack from the southwest. Our aim is only to live. To live to fight tyranny.'

The other William, similar in temperament to his older and more experienced counterpart was at Margaret's house, and was also planning. It was early in the morning, the sun had not yet risen, but he wanted the battle and felt frustrated by the domesticity he had drifted into, the day before. He had already decided that he would exemplify bravery in battle, would get noticed by Captain Thompson and would undoubtedly be invited to ride with the

Levellers. He needed a horse, but he was certain that he would be granted one by Death. He didn't think about the fate of his sister. He loved her but she was not his future. Anyway Brilliana was independent of mind and will. Nathaniel Elkin seemed a good sort, but he was weakened by his time in prison, and William did not think he would be much help. Perhaps he would stay with Brilliana he mused, and glanced over to where the two of them were chatting by the cold, sharp window. He was motivated by justice rather than compassion, and often engrossed himself in a morality tale, where he was the hero ever proved right in his judgement and choices. He grabbed his satchel and, motioning to Margaret, the two of them left through the gloom of the archway into the still dark street.

Nathaniel's hair disguised the secret of his eyes, hiding them from her like a veil. Brilliana brushed it away. She could hear her voice telling him about when she had met Elber Choke whilst getting sugar for her mother. Nathaniel's grey eyes were like fish eyes she thought to herself, inscrutable and cold. She wondered if she could make him laugh and she tried to mimic some of the characters from her childhood. He smiled at her but remained self-contained, like a tight-lidded bottle allowing only sips of water to be spilt from it. He has edges, she thought, joined up edges to his soul that allow nothing out. She wondered if he allowed anything in. Brilliana was sure footed and had decided that she may choose to love Nathaniel, for he was good looking enough. She knew that he wouldn't refuse her and, like Pandora, she wanted to see into that vessel. She suspected it was full of charm, wit,

CHAPTER 10

love and passion. She didn't suspect it might be empty, for she was only young.

Brilliana's imp-like warmth gently heated Nathaniel's skin after his recent life in the cold, dark prison. He loved her already and longed for her soft companionship. He didn't know her, but liked her laughter and her adventure. He was less sure about William who he felt looked down on him after his time in prison. He felt despised. He had no voice, and little understanding of what had actually happened to him, but Brilliana was the soft surface he had been looking for. William had the dream and ambition that Nathaniel had been jealous of, and, despite the feelings of inadequacy, he wanted to stay with William to learn how to be a man of ideals. Nathaniel had little pride left, but enough intelligence to understand that in this brother and sister he could find the answers he had left his mother for.

Brilliana laid a soft hand on Nathaniel's arm and he smiled at her and laid his still-tired head in her lap. He failed to appreciate that it was Brilliana who had the ideals, William simply wanted adventure and to prove himself. At this moment Nathaniel was a seventeenth century man, with the prejudicial view of women that entailed. That view would undergo some change. She kissed the top of his head and raising his head he stared deeply into her eyes and the hard edges between them blurred.

Chapter 11

William and Margaret strode into town, fixed as arrows and welcoming their fate. The Levellers' horses were poring at the cobbles as if trying to uproot them for ammunition, snorting at their failure with ears pricked, and listening wildly for danger. The men skulked around their horses, chatting and chewing on dry crusts of bread, eyes tired from another sleepless night. William spoke to a few men hidden in the early morning mist. They were enthusiastic about his offer of allegiance, and he and Margaret were rushed over to a tall man with mouse-brown hair.

They were in the grounds of the castle where the Levellers were focused. 'So you want to join us then? To fight for equality and democracy?' William nodded and Margaret introduced herself to the man. He knew her son's name and immediately bowed low as if to brush the ground before her with his own hair. 'Come with me.'

CHAPTER 11

Smoke still fluttered up from the shacks in the moat and ditch of the castle. The mottled brown men and women were intent on commerce, even within a crisis, and shouted about their goods and their prices throughout the night. They hoped that these new commanders would feed their families. Free trade was impervious to political battles, being unchallenged by either Cromwell or Levellers. Margaret and William ignored this goblin market and climbed up the grey stone steps. A huge fireplace spluttered out Brownian-motioned smoke, hazing their view. Colonel William Thompson met them and shook their hands heartily. He had met Margaret's son once and sympathetically showed her to the largest and softest chair. 'Have you heard from your son, Margaret?' Margaret shook her head, 'I have not, Colonel Thompson, but I presume he is alive. I just wait for our victory and his release.' Margaret nodded and William Thompson stretched a thin smile.

He did not think there could be victory and he did not want to raise false hope. Yet at the same time, honesty would not inspire even a desperate man to ride with him, and he needed men to ride with him. He needed more men than he had, to stand with him, in order to avoid complete annihilation. 'We are grateful for your support. We expect Cromwell's men today or tomorrow, and it will be fierce. Do you think many in the town will raise arms with us?'

'I will.' William Barebone could not resist making himself known to his hero. Colonel Thompson smiled and shouted out that the man should be given a horse. It was an overweening gesture as there were not enough horses, and the Levellers had been deep in conversation the day before about whether stealing the horses in the town could be justified. Colonel Thompson had sent out a few men to barter with the locals using the gold they had taken from the castle vaults, to see if they could buy horses. If the locals would not sell, because of principle or price, then he could see no option but to take them if they were to avoid certain death. Luckily the men had returned with some horses purchased with the castle gold.

The locals were, however, mostly loyal to Cromwell, and not easily persuaded by these traitorous pirates. They had not sold their best horses to them. Some of the more eager Levellers thought that stealing some of the finer horses could still be justified and Thompson privately agreed that having strong horses was essential if they were to actually win the battle.

The extra nags they had bought already, however, were probably good enough to ensure that Cromwell's men would not destroy them within minutes of the start of battle. This would enable a weaker plan of escape to be enacted. Thompson realised that if they angered the locals by stealing from them, then the locals could turn against them in the battle and actively fight on Cromwell's side. This would pin them in the town, surrounding them on all sides, and would lead to their inevitable demise. If they didn't anger them, then the locals may let them escape, at least. The question was whether he was going to send these men to their honourable deaths or give them an escape route. Colonel Thompson was decent and kind and

CHAPTER 11

he decided on the escape route, gave up any notion of victory, and ordered that no horses were to be stolen.

A scrawny-twig man dressed in leathery green escorted William and Margaret out of the keep as Thompson had been suddenly called away to his men, thus avoiding an unwelcome discussion with the mother of the martyred Thomas Prince. He had been unable to meet her eye. The green- leathered soldier held the reins of a bone-pitted grey horse that he passed reluctantly over to William. The ragged three walked back through the town towards Margaret's house, excited and scared in equal measure. William was lost in a daydream world of honour and bravery where he proudly revealed himself to be a leader of principle. Margaret's thoughts were of her son and her clear perception that Thompson had never mentioned a victory, and had looked tired and pensive.

William marched into the kitchen of Margaret's house, and saw his sister and Nathanial entwined together on a chair like a bundle of old washing. They were both asleep. William wanted to wake them and shout madly about his conversation with Colonel Thompson, but he felt strangely reticent and private suddenly. Brilliana stirred and looked over at him, jumping cat-like onto her feet and smoothing down her edges. William found he couldn't speak and Brilliana bustled with the kettle on the fire that had smouldered low. Margaret carried some potatoes towards the table and started chopping them ready for breakfast.

Pensive clouds gathered about them as their soft-focused naïveté slowly evaporated, leaving a harder focus to their surroundings. Each had experienced the real within the ideal; William had understood the impossibility of the venture within each tired gesture of Thompson, and had quickly and desperately filled each doubt with courage solid enough to hold onto the dream. Brilliana realised that as soon as she felt herself in love with Nathaniel, she had cut herself from him suddenly and coldly as if trying to rescue herself from drowning. It was like paddling in the white-water river, before running scared up the pebble beach as foam waves tried to catch her and drag her back in. She did not want to be devoured by him.

Both had discovered a serious heart. They could see the details now through the stretched translucent surface of mysterious ideal. They could see the bones through the skin. The detail was complex and immoral. There were gains and losses. The gloss of ideal hid the glory and the treachery of humanity, within a victory could be a personal defeat, and within happiness could be personal suffering. That to win equality for men would mean killing men. That to win love could mean losing love and could mean losing oneself to another. They realised the individual sacrifice demanded by the universal good and that each decision and each choice was a compromise, and that the Devil did, indeed, lie in the detail.

Chapter 12

Brilliana and Nathaniel shrugged off the haunted feeling as the sun climbed slowly over the horizon, and they meandered hand in hand through the cobbled streets. William had sent them scouting whilst he rested at the house, and they were alert for any sign of Cromwell's men. They felt alive. Warmth spread through Nathaniel's chest, like a hot spring of joy warming him in the cold morning. The girl beside him danced and swung on his arm, tripping him and pulling him this way and that. She appeared chaotic but in truth she was his puppeteer, delighting in her ability to unbalance him at her whim. He didn't mind. His thoughts were, as usual, basic and honest. He felt unreservedly glad by his fortune.

For the first time in his life Nathaniel had someone to love and someone to live for. He had someone to fight for. He was no longer alone, but was part of humanity. The hope for softness had been nurtured into a dream of happiness, and now he found himself willing a future, rather than simply resisting a present. Brilliana looked at the world like it was a shining, fragile cobweb: she, like Nathaniel felt part of it, a strand in the web with meaning and purpose, the meaning being life itself. For Brilliana, however, this was not a new thought but had been conjured in the cauldron of trees in her childhood.

'I believe in equality, Nathaniel, but it angers me that the Levellers don't include women in their demands for extension of the franchise, for the vote. I want it, and need it to include women. I don't understand why Levellers are happy with these leftover bits of inequality: inequality between men and women, and economic inequality. If William has all the jewels in the world and yet you have nothing, how could that be real equality? Doesn't the very idea of equality necessitate economic equality as well as political and legal equality? So you have the same Leveller freedoms as William, the same freedom to vote and choose the leaders, the same freedom to be punished by the law for a crime, but why stop there? Why shouldn't William share his jewels? He'd still have some, but so would you. What is wrong with that Nathaniel? I don't want people to starve whilst others grow fat.' She had the tone of an insolent child.

Nathaniel struggled to remember some of the conversations from the inn to answer Brilliana's question, but was at a loss. He did understand money, however, and something about value. He was puffed up with his own virgin importance and gripped in the embrace of amour-propre. Her childish tone talked to the father in him.

CHAPTER 12

Nathaniel was in error because Brilliana had looked at his soul and thought it would be a mirror. She was looking for a friend and playmate, not a master. He replied, 'Well jewels cost money and people work to earn money to buy jewels. The people who work hardest earn the most and buy the best jewels. Why would people work hard if everyone had the same?' Brilliana listened and felt her second fluttering disappointment in love. 'So you're saying that there has to be some inequality?' She was not looking into a mirror after all.

'Yes, and if someone ploughs a field and works hard doing that, they should be entitled to the fruits of that labour, the produce that grows in that field and have rights to sell that produce if they want to.' He felt delighted, and puffed up further. Both were lost in a maze of mutual misunderstanding, and so they didn't hear the footsteps behind them. They did hear the sharp voice cut through their disillusionment like a knife, 'and I saved you, gave you my water and bread which you took without payment, which means that I own you.' Elber Choke's tongue rasped at them and stopped them short. They felt rough hands on their shoulders as the sky went ink-black.

Choke paid the six hefty men, who had helped him carry the two bodies, with some of the gold coins saved from the Levellers' generosity. He kicked Nathaniel on the floor. He had his two acquisitions, delivered to a beer cellar below an inn on the Market Square. He didn't know their names, they were just objects to him, objects that could be bought and sold. Vagrants. The air was damp and smelt of melancholic nights barely remembered. They were tightly bound and he wasn't concerned about any fight back or resistance. He hadn't counted on the girl, but she looked strong enough that someone would buy her to work for them, and was poor enough that no one would miss her. He had a few more purchases to make before driving them to the Bristol port to sell them for indentured labour. They were now further in debt to him as he was generous and left bread and water. He bound them and went on his way.

To the south of the town an explosion crumpled the morning air and the black-eyed Puritans dropped to their knees. Cromwell's men were at the river that girdled the castle walls. They were earlier than expected. Margaret stretched her hand out and grasped William's. She had earned her stout heart through years of absence and loss but she feared for this boy and his sister whom she had grown fond of. She had not really noticed Nathaniel, as he lacked the ideals of the other two, ideals that that kept her heart strong and had kept her alive these years.

William stood up and pulled his satchel across his body. 'It's time, Margaret'. His stomach lurched and he thought he would be sick. This was the moment he had waited for his whole life. Time stopped in silence and the earth held its breath as he scattered into the eternal. Moments later the wind gusted and woke William, now high on his horse and galloping towards the castle. He was locked into his fate.

Chapter 13

Brilliana felt a rough anger at her wrists and realised the heavy damp rope was being undone. They had not been tied up for long. A young girl crouched at her side, lit golden by a lamp made crooked by the cobbles. She wore a grey cap and apron and her voice lilted with the memory of lyric Irish landscapes. 'The town's on fire and the army is on us. The landlord got some Leveller gold as payment for you two, but I just can't see you die down here like rats. They, and everyone else in this godforsaken town have gone to pretend to fight, which means they're hiding in their friends cellars out of the town, whilst I guard the inn, so they'll not know I let you go free. Just run out of here quietly you two and don't come back. I'll say some Levellers running from the army got you loose. I hate with bitter torment that Elber Choke, the miserable slaver. The Kings men stole me from my mother four years ago, in

Drogheda. Choke sold me to the landlord here as an unpaid servant. I sleep over there. '

She pointed to a bundle of bitter-brown blankets, damp from the beery atmosphere, as a pneumatic cough ratcheted through her thin bones. Darkness gloomed her pallid complexion as she was reminded of her fragility and her mortality.

'That is terrible. Are you a slave? What is your name?' Brilliana spoke with the same profound sorrow she had felt as a child at seeing a stare-eyed rabbit twitching in a cold-teethed trap. She had refused the rancid stew that had resulted, and was beaten for it.

'My name is Anne,' she whispered as another cough tore through her body. 'I'm not a slave, I am a servant. I am beaten and abused every minute of every day. But unlike the slaves I should be free in a year or so." She winced. The black African slaves, they never get free.' She looked at the floor.

'You are fed and sheltered,' Nathaniel's voice broke in to the pity like a robber, stealing the shared compassion. Anne nodded in agreement. Brilliana felt heat surge into her heart and she stared at Nathaniel. 'You cannot be saying that she should be grateful Nathaniel, to be allowed no choice over her actions, no choice in what she does and when, because she is just lucky to eat dry bread every day. Freedom is a dignity even afforded to animals in nature and should be the natural right of every human.'

Nathaniel stared at the floor. 'I saw my mother and sisters in grim sigh each day as hungered fingers clutched at their

Chapter 13

shrunken stomachs. I know not whether they are dead or alive now, but they could have been better served if they were kept like Anne. Brilliana, you talk about economic equality as more important than political equality, but yet you don't understand poverty.' He turned towards Anne, 'and the necessity of survival.'

'I understand poverty Nathaniel,' Brilliana breathed indignation, 'But I don't and won't accept it. We must fight against all enslavement, to money or man. Tyranny takes many forms; the political tyranny of Cromwell, the tyranny of slavery, tyrannies to the people and land in enclosures, and to animals in the trap, as well as the tyranny of the mob. Anything or anyone that usurps my own sovereignty is wrong Nathaniel. Anyone who usurps your sovereignty is wrong. A person starving is the result of enslavement to money. Money is also a tyranny and a threat to my sovereignty.'

'Money is freedom, Brilliana, and we should work hard to gain it. The Levellers are right, there must be political equality amongst men for justice and fairness to be served, but economic equality cannot be welcomed because it is that very inequality that makes us all work hard. We work hard to gain more and to escape poverty, and we must work hard for progress to be made.

I am against servitude and against slavery for men, because men should win or lose capital by their own actions, but it is different for women. Men have always governed women, because that's the natural order, and Anne has only given up her freedom to a master rather than a husband. Women will not have political freedom in our lifetime, and neither will they have economic freedom. It's just the way of things. You talk about sovereignty but you have no sovereignty as a woman, because God has not granted that.' Nathaniel's coarse words had been learnt at the feet of his father; a safe, deep place that his mind had fled to in the face of danger.

Brilliana felt shaken, as if a door had just slammed into her face. She was locked out. Anne had slumped on her bed and was not listening, as the voices only added to her despair. Nathaniel looked down at Brilliana and reached out his hand to hers. She welcomed his touch from within her confusion, as reassurance that he loved her still. Her great-aunt, with whom she had spent most of her childhood, had not shared the tyrannous view of women held by the majority. She and William were fortunate that they had escaped the confines of this particular prison, but she now realised that she was not free to enter the world as an equal. She was shocked at the casual brutality. 'We must go,' whispered Nathaniel urgently.

Anne waved the two friends away, not wanting to risk the adventure in ill health. Nathaniel felt the dents in his wrists made by the rope, scooped Brilliana's hand into his and clambered up the stone steps. They blinked at the light and ran like blinded children as fast as they could. They heard blasts and shouts in the distance that searched their heads and their eyes, and as sensations returned they drew to a stop, panting in a shop doorway. 'Brilliana, the fighting's begun, I must join them.'

Nathaniel's gaze fixated towards the dragon fire-breath licking the sky over the square, solid castle keep. She felt confused and scared. She looked around as if seeing more of the picture would help her know what to do. Nathaniel bounced on his toes. 'I'll see you at Margaret's,' and he fluttered away like a moth towards the light, leaving Brilliana cold and alone.

Bitter tears jabbed at her eyes, burning sour down her cheeks, and she slumped pitifully in the doorway. Nathaniel thought she could play no part in the battle because she was a woman. Yet she had heard a tale of a farmer's daughter who had raised a rifle at Marston Moor, and she was certain that this woman was not the only one who had fought with men. She felt humiliated by Nathaniel's clumsy action and was made insignificant by him. Overpowered by virgin emotion, by a love that she was unused to, she was wrong-footed and unsure of herself and she did not follow him. She pitied herself in this surrender. She cursed him again because she was not as important to him as his battle glory and she felt a petty jealousy of the battle as if a rival lover. These pities were gilded by a sense of unfairness at his tacit assumption that she would wait for him, because he was of singular importance for her. She felt deeply sorry for herself, and wept in the doorway like a child that had lost her favourite doll.

Chapter 14

Sitting at her kitchen table, straight backed and tense, Margaret was absorbed in the thunderstorm tempest around her but the deep bursts of cannon were muffled, and the light was dull. Her house felt strangely still, and silent, as though in the eye of the storm, as though not of the world. She felt like she was fainting as she held Thompson's unread Common Agreement pamphlet in her hand. Grey hair floated around her face like a cloud of smoke captured from the Putney Debates and wound around her hair in remembrance of her son.

Her mind was wandering again into a murky realm, where time refracted like light through water. This was the place her son had rescued her from, but he was absent now and she was alone. She was scared, but could not stop herself from walking towards the sound of rushing water; she could see it sliding turquoise over rocks. She felt it lapping at her feet, ice-cold, and she swam deep into the depth of

CHAPTER 14

emerald green. Below the surface appeared visions of men: her husband and son, as well as others less familiar, but known to her, and those stranger men talked as they did in Putney. They conjured up demands for liberty and religious tolerance, spelling out that the power lay with the people, not the King, and demanded fairness for the poor.

She saw her son turning before her eyes into a boy of four, his hair now a mass of blonde curls. He lay in her father's house, playing with a favourite fruitwood spinning-top. He lay flat on his stomach, kicking his soft, plump feet whilst watching it spin and turn in eternal gyre. She called to him, but there was no sound, and her mouth filled with water and she panicked at the suffocation. She spat out the water in desperation, coughing hard spheres onto the floor, which landed as round, glass eyes. The eyes poured out of her mouth, hundreds and hundreds, covering the floor like a thousand peacock feathers. They stared blankly, and coldly at her son, as they fell onto the floor beside him. He turned to smile at her with his broad carefree smile. She sobbed in pitiful sorrow at the coldness and the hardness of the eyes staring in stark comparison with the sweetness and softness of her son. The sharp knock at the door rescued her from the opiate illusion, and drying her tears, she bustled towards the sound.

John Barebone believed he had marched in glorious rapture towards Northampton, like God's soldier, fighting demons along the way. He had certainly been fighting with demons. He had left his home shortly after his daughter, he remembered closing the wooden door behind him, but then time stopped its relentless routine and started lurching around, mirroring the movements of his own body. He found himself sitting under a blush-barked yew tree, it's beckoning fingers sweeping the needle floor, and he heard the sound of an angel singing ethereal notes from another world. He felt himself swimming in the song itself, he was saturated for centuries in Ariel's harmony, before he suddenly woke, standing soldier-straight in a grassy clearing. The grass was breathing and swaying in rhythm with the song, and the stars were high in the indigo sky, lines joining the constellations as if he were sheltering under a star map. Nature felt gratuitous and capacious, fulsome and ripe, it was too much to bear and he felt hot tears wash down his face.

Looking up at the stars, John Barebone felt the sudden panic as electricity firing up his backbone. The stars were an illusion, nothing more than a picture of stars, the grass was a picture, he was in a painting, and nothing was real. His panic turned to rage and he tore clumps of grass up with his bare hands. Inspecting the turf he saw ants running down the stems; black and bulbous, pouring out of the mud, and they were running down his arm, and covering it in black demon snakeskin.

He awoke to feel the cold stone of a house leaning out onto his body, and he realised that he was in town. The song disappeared with the panic, replaced by the words of God himself, comfortingly caressing his ear. He was chosen by God and he could no longer feel the gnawing of hunger in his grey distended belly, or the cuts and blue-eyed bruises on his legs and arms where that demonic daughter had

CHAPTER 14

attacked him. God was talking to him, a constant certainty, whispering in his ear, telling him the secrets of the devils and the demons in the town. The smell of sulphur was overpowering to John as he wandered the town, and tears poured down his face. The people were bent, without limb and feature, with twisted, boggle-eyed faces, devouring each other as in a Brueghel depiction of Hell. Disgust wrapped him up and then God himself told him to go to that house at that time.

The open door revealed to Margaret a strange, swollen, wet-faced man, smeared in dirt and carrying a bible. Margaret intuited danger and tried to slam the heavy door shut, but the door was slow to respond and she fell back into the kitchen glow. Fingers grabbed her throat, clutching at her windpipe as if to pull it out of her neck. 'Where is she? My daughter is the demon Lilith herself, God himself speaks to me and has told me she is here.'

Margaret gasped as if to reply, but she was too slow, and John Barebone holding tight her throat and pulling her towards him like a rag doll, slammed her smoky head into the window frame, again and again. Her skull crumpled like a cloud revealing black blood ooze where her mind had been. Her pale hands pushed at his black coat, but it was like pushing a shadow, for material substance had long since left him. Her death was sordid and violent, and the Earth shuddered, hanging her gloomy veil over the town, muting the battle sound, as the ghosts behind the veil screamed in pain.

Margaret's thoughts, now free from her mind, gasped at the oxygen and floated high into the sky where they flew with the birds, before dropping like dandelion heads into the whirlpools of air above the town. For the next few months they danced around the roofs and alleyways, blown away by the bare, blonde children playing with their rainbow stones, before they landed lightly in the minds of a few lucky, radical souls.

In that moment, where Margaret's head first became clouded and the shadow fell over her, she dreamed of her husband in the wild flower meadow where they had laughed as children, and danced as newlyweds. He held her tight in his arms and he smiled at her, and she finally drowned in his eyes.

Chapter 15

Nathaniel felt he could conquer the world. He had never run so swiftly or so sure-footedly. The smoke and the thunder called him like a siren and he ran without thought into the storm. As he turned the corner he heard the men scream like howling animals and the horses' hooves fear-stamp on cobble, but he felt no fear. He gripped a wooden pole in both hands, gained without reason and with absent mind, and swept through the north gate of the castle and over the wooden drawbridge. Inside the walls it was bedlam. Ahead he saw the battle dance of the horses and heard the shouts of men amid the thunderclap shots that seemed to encourage them on, as if in a dark and grim play.

'Nathaniel, you're here.' William sat high on his horse, his face haloed by the sunshine. He was heroic in the midst of fear, like a knight of old, as he smiled down at Nathaniel. William shrugged towards the steps to the right of them. 'There are no more horses but you could climb the keep and fire one of the mortars that Thompson's men found at the castle.' The mortars were barrel-like weapons, tiny cannons filled with explosives that could be fired out into the ground beyond. Nathaniel climbed the steps like an immortal to the Heaven of the keep and surveyed the ground outside the castle walls.

Within only one heartbeat, only one glance, fear clutched at his stomach, and the world turned upside down. He felt the world as burning pain and blister, and wrapped in sulphur and smoke he felt himself to be more in Hell than in Heaven. Aside the slow churning river were two hundred horses or more, and men, with cannons and muskets, exploding the air about them in an arrogant anthem. Sickness swept over him in tidal waves as he bent double to load the mortar.

The midday sunlight masked the shadow of death, making it shine in fury, appearing glorious and epic to the soldiers below. Nathaniel, from his high point, saw only the shadow. He smelt the stench of the fireworks, filling his nostrils and his head like thick sand. His ears were deafened by the sordid sounds, which was welcome sensory relief for him. This was a dismal display that showered burnt flesh and torment into the world around. The horses twitched their demise in sorrowful insignificance, collected by fate; their lives sacrificed to the battle of ideas.

The castle provided excellent advantage. Thompson and a few others, William being one, were huddled within the walls. Other soldiers had manned the battlements and walls and were firing muskets at the aggressors. Nathaniel

Chapter 15

could see brave pike-men, some on horses, by the river, face-to-face with their new enemy: with men who had been their friends and comrades just a month before. It was pitiful to witness the loss of humanity, which was given away so lightly. Death should be tortured and agonised over. Here it was dispatched easily and without thought. If they did not have the advantage of the castle they would have been dead within minutes. As it was, it might take hours, and with that thought his mind froze.

Nathaniel was rendered impotent by futility and meaninglessness. It wrapped itself like a snake around his body, squeezing the breath from his bones. He was unable to fire the mortar anymore; he was profoundly terrified and trembled uncontrollably. He did not fear death, as much as fear a life that was futile. He needed meaning but it was not to be found in the chaos of war. He had been wrong.

Below him the horses whinnied as William Thompson spoke. 'We are outnumbered friends, but this is not a place to die. The river beaches the tyrants and we need to flee to our next place of refuge. We must speak our words and the people must hear them, for that is our purpose today and tomorrow. We shall ride out the north gate and towards Wellingborrow town to the east as the army will not be there. There we can get rest and parade our pamphlet. I will stay with ten men beside me, whilst you ride out. Those without horse must blend back into the crowd. Do you hear me? I will follow when you are gone.'

Touching his face as he spoke, Thompson traced the lines and marks. Each line was a death mark of the men he had killed for Cromwell, and those death marks etched his face as a map of torment and despair. The horror of killing had been justified in good conscience and ideal but Cromwell's betrayal carved them deeper and more painfully into his skin. Thompson had no choice but to run, because more death was just more death, gratuitous and meaningless. The only thing that could save his soul and his conscience from his own actions were the words of honour that he had written in his pamphlet. He hated Cromwell for turning him into a killer without reason, but he wanted to save himself.

William heard Thompson's words and scoured the keep for Nathaniel. He found him bent over the mortar, his face powdered white with gunpowder and fear. Nathaniel collapsed into William's arms and William felt his cold, clammy flesh, fish-scaled like his eyes. He wrapped his coat around him to stop the shiver. 'Come on Nathaniel, we must leave now'. William was not feared by the battle, he felt truly alive with idea and conviction. He felt immortal and Godly. William did not suffer from compassion, which had been beaten out of him in his childhood. He understood justice: his mind like scales that weighed up every event in terms of fairness and rightness. He was a Leveller, and a future leader of men. Nathaniel used his wooden pole to help him down the steps; they both clambered onto William's granite-grey mare and galloped together towards Margaret's house.

Chapter 16

The inn smelt like a rancid tomb as Elber Choke ducked his head under the stiff oaken beam by the door. It was deserted like the streets behind him. Like foxes gone to earth the good people of Northampton had run to their houses at the sound of gunshot and had firmly locked their doors behind them. Choke lazily shuffled down to the cellar, his mole eyes blinking in the gloom where he quickly perceived that his goods had been stolen, or had escaped. The spiral of rope lay flaccid by the barrels of beer. Choke pursed his lips in annoyance and let out a strange hiss, like a kettle about to boil. He glowered at the scene before him and cursed the landlord whom he had paid with Leveller gold to look after his property. Anne Erkeson lay wrapped in her blankets, praying to her Catholic God that He would not demand her to cough and reveal her hiding place. Her breath swept over her in shallow waves and tiny beads of sweat broke out over her skin like a pox.

Choke, however, was nothing if not an opportunist. He did not understand principle and his anger at the landlord was short-lived, as it was not motivated by any sense of natural justice, only by a narcissistic resentment that someone had got the better of him. Instead his quick, rat-like mind saw the barrels of beer in the cellar and set to work carrying them hunchbacked to the top of the stairs and out to the horse and cart that were waiting. Nine, ten barrels would fetch good pennies and were compensation for his loss. After thirty backbreaking minutes, Choke drove the horse up the north road, bound for Market Harborough and away from the skirmish to the south.

Redemption had been granted to Anne Erkeson that day. God had forgiven her because He had granted her the victory over this man. She shared the guilt of original sin with the Puritans, but for her it was not to be lived as punishment every day (despite her conditions), but was more of a universal fact for everyone, including Choke, and including her masters; a fact that could not be escaped. Anne Erkeson made the best of her life, lightly giving herself up to fate. Now she hugged herself tightly, praying that salvation would follow after the bloody-eyed beating she would receive from the landlord for letting the beer be stolen.

The bitter-eyed landlord of the inn squinted at his companions in another part of the town, a part of the town safely away from the battle. He was not a natural ally of the Puritan but was passionate in his support for the tyrant. He was terrified of the anarchy that might ensue if the Levellers took control. He had a great deal to lose. 'Aye, the Levellers will ransack my inn,' he spoke to his friends with a sour note in his voice, 'But they will be sincerely sorry when they do, and not just because they'll come across that dry spun girl I left there.' He let out a laugh that hovered in his throat, inspiring fear in his friends, rather than mirth. 'I have poisoned those barrels of beer in my cellar, they were old anyway, and no loss compared to what will be if those pirates win. When those Levellers drink my beer they will die like the dogs they are.' His friends let out the deep growling laughter of approval. 'Do you think Cromwell will reward my service?' He said, 'Perhaps I will become a Lord?' He revelled in his cunning. 'Just don't forget and drink it yourself,' laughed his friends in hopeful mockery.

Chapter 17

Salvation is rare and hard sought but self-pity poisons a mind like cheap wine that is easy to find, and Brilliana was drunk on it. She staggered down the alleyways towards Margaret's house, hardly noticing the empty streets around her, clutching her ears. Her tears had dried and she felt empty. The absence of joy lies in hollow emptiness and nothingness rather than in sadness. Sadness nurtures a hope of something better, a particle of joy, an implicit connection with one's environment, whilst emptiness is the realisation of one's absolute separation from everything; oneself as absence, cold and total. This was how Brilliana felt, without joy and without sadness.

Her destination was captured in the eye of a tempest, as if outside time itself, the natural laws of nature were suspended. The house could no longer be apprehended within any normal understanding of space and time; everything happened instantly and could not be seen, but

CHAPTER 17

yet was seen and happened over years. Time itself stretched and shrank space at whim, playing with space like a magician.

The house was a place of dread and foul vision, where crimson mercury leaked onto the stone floor like a river. It was as hot as a bread oven and sweat poured off the brow of John Barebone. The house was full of people shouting and cursing; hobby-horses poured feverishly at flagstones, tousle-haired children sobbed with starvation; their ribs burning white through flesh, women burnt black at Satanic stakes and one single man hanging by a noose, neck broken and tongue distended, gloated from up high. Each visitor sneered at John Barebone, and he clutched at his head, as if to tear it off.

Margaret stretched herself out in the wild flower meadow. She was smothered in fragrant incense and was wrapped in silvery silk gifted from the silkworm and spider. Lofty poppies nodded at the breeze, agreeing with unheard words, whilst azure cornflowers bristled in glee at the joke. Grasses brushed Margaret as if sweeping sin away, serious in obligation, they bowed their heads and looked sternly at the cornflowers, which ignored them in their tremble.

John Barebone flung each window and door in the house open, gasping for breath. 'I CAN'T HEAR YOU LORD,' he screamed. God's voice had become a tiny whisper now, like the sound of flies buzzing on a golden yellow cream curdled in summertime. The sound was a constant companion but John could not hear the words. He flung open windows and doors as if this would give him clarity.

The visitors screeched away like banshees, and there was a brief souring silence before the marks mottled on the kitchen wall transformed into faces before him. These faces dripped with fear, burning in a fury of fire. The walls pulsed and breathed as Margaret lost her own pulse and breath to them. He grabbed a knife and carved at his arms like totems, deep crucifix cuts into sinewy flesh, red in alarm.

As Brilliana walked into the kitchen she saw only patches of colour before her, reds and browns and something black at the centre. She had no words to describe the scene, no schema to understand it or to know it. The reds were raw and damp and were mopped onto Margaret's twisted body. In the heart she saw the black, deadlight of her father and heard the sound of a knife falling onto the table. She felt an iron weight hit her hard in the chest and she fell into the deadlight wormhole of her father's soul.

Brilliana Barebone was swaddled in snakes that emerged from deep within her mind, hissing and circling around her head; snakes with poisoned tongues that licked at John Barebone. Toads climbed clumsily on her leg and arm and John felt sick with the Sycorax-stench of sulphur that emanated from her. He fell onto her, but his skin prickled hotly in disgust and he jumped up, brushing wildly at the contamination that soaked into his legs and arms.

Flying proudly up to the ceiling, she hovered high, scouting the ground beneath her. She was circling in tree branches high in Prospero's grove. She recognised the unicorn tree and the dragon tree and she saw herself sitting astride the unicorn as a child, galloping gleefully through the forest. In a clearing she could see her father, looking savagely like the Minotaur, lost in the maze of his mind, devouring men's corpses for sustenance. She swooped towards him; she grabbed the knife and plunged it hard into his tough Puritan, patriarchal skin.

John Barebone saw white-horsed light, flickering like sunlight through lace. He heard God's voice calling to him again, clear as the bright bell that rang him to church. God was welcoming him. John Barebone noticed that he was clutching a star map in his hand. He felt irritation scabies-scratch at his thin skin, and in tormented distraction he fastidiously tore the map into a million, tiny pieces. The light faded without him noticing, and suddenly blinked out. He was alone in the dark.

Chapter 18

Nathaniel and William jumped down from the horse and William ran into the house. He stopped dead at the sight before him. Margaret lay slumped under the window, black-blood pasting her grey hair to her blanched face, her eyes closed in peace. He saw Brilliana sitting calmly cross-legged by the fireplace. Their father lay stiff on the floor in funeral black, with a single silver handle, like a fish-fin, rising from his chest. William had no love for his father who had been a tiresome pedant as a child. He and Brilliana had escaped the chores by running and hiding in the woods, but he had often found him and beaten him. William still bore the scars on his back from brutal thrashing in the name of the Lord. William was not a sentimental man. The chores had given him a practical way of apprehending the world, and the beatings had extinguished any superfluous emotional life. He

CHAPTER 18

understood what had happened. He grabbed Brilliana's hand and quietly led her outside.

Brilliana saw Nathaniel's dark curls, soft and forgiving and she similarly curled into his arms, burying her face in his chest. As he held her, she felt sadness and joy burn from within once more, and spasm one desperate sob as her emotion released. He held her tightly as if she were a life-raft, for he was also scared of drowning. They stood gripped together in silence as William packed food and water onto the horse, and they set off, William holding the horse whilst Brilliana and Nathaniel clutched together for safety.

It was ten miles to Wellingborrow, mostly through farmland and wood. They left Northampton in late afternoon and were walking quickly to make the town before nightfall. The track was well worn, straight and mostly flat, with a gentle rise and fall that felt like a rocking cradle, soothing their journey. They passed a group of three weary and ramshackle cottages and stopped on a nearby bench to eat the bread and drink the watery beer. The people blinked out of the cottages and stared silently, they seemed to be modelled out of the thick clay of the earth beneath their feet, and their faces resembled the root vegetables they dug out of the ground. The clothes they wore were only the rags of a scarecrow, yet the friends felt the peasants gaze as cold judgement, and so they hurried their food down, walking on whilst still empty. They wondered where Thompson and the Levellers had gone. Nathaniel felt abandoned and alone;

discarded. He swallowed the dark despair that gripped his mind; his impotence in battle still haunted him.

The clutch of cold fear that had gripped Brilliana was loosening with each step. The warm evening sun stroked her skin, brightening her expression as well as the colours around. The greens and reds were glowing vivid and intense, causing her to gasp wide-eyed at their terrible beauty. She felt she was newborn, seeing the world for the first time. Nathaniel was still wrapped up in his gloom and so she decided to walk with William. She told him of their kidnapping at the hands of Elber Choke and talked quickly and indignantly about the Irish girl who had rescued them, before they fell back into sombre silence again. They did not have the words to describe their more recent feelings and they lacked the words to give thought to their crimes. Some emotions lie in a transcendent realm beyond words, and for Brilliana they would never be expressed in her life. The loss and the terror could drip slowly away. This was another fortune, and in it laid her survival.

Brilliana had listened to the scratch and chirp of the birds through the late afternoon and evening, whilst the trees had bristled in the breeze that blew over them. Now the dusk played in the shadows, excited at the thought of night, as the friends neared the town of Wellingborrow. The late evening was wearily warm, as the green-spine trees of the spinney to the left of the track teased them to rest. William led his horse to a pool of water and the grey mare snuffled at the long damp grass beside it.

William Thompson lay dead at the foot of a Chestnut tree in the spinney, some way from where the companions

CHAPTER 18

rested. Cromwell's soldiers had killed him hours earlier; soldiers from the army he had once fought with, and had thought of as brothers. He had raced ten miles away from the soldiers, until his heart felt like it would explode. In the end his heart had surrendered and the joy had left his body. He had killed a couple of the soldiers, before finally succumbing to a bullet of musket lead, which lodged like a black curse close to his heart. He was shot in the back as he had dreamed he would be.

Nathaniel saw something white, like a lantern in the night, and called William over. The pamphlets were scattered like chilly candles and they led the frightened friends to Thompson's body. William carefully gathered the pamphlets up and held them like a baby. He felt the Levellers idea biting his heart, a beautiful pain, sharp and honest. He felt sorrow flood through his body, drowning his weariness.

"I think that the poorest he that is in England, hath a life to live as the greatest he, and therefore truly, sir, I think it is clear to every man that is to live under a government ought first by his own consent to put himself under that government."* He heard Thompson's soft, honest voice in his ear, repeating these words to him, talking about freedom of conscience, of tolerance. The tyrant Cromwell had heard the hissing voice of God telling him to act as a king, telling him that men were not ready to rule themselves. His authority had turned to a tyranny and he and Heaven had betrayed humanity and Thompson. William cursed that man and the God that spoke to him and made him necessary. Nathaniel turned Thompson's body over. His face was carved like stone, the pain was solid and the hope had gone.

'We need to rest, William. The day is gone, but tomorrow will be fine. We will take the pamphlets and distribute them William. His voice will not die'. Brilliana stroked her brother's arm as she stroked his mind with these words. She could see the distress in his face and worried for them all if he were to crumble. The violence of the shock she had felt in Margaret's house had matched the violence of her father's death, but in every footstep that distanced her from that blooded body, she had lost the intensity of feeling. It seemed like an absurd dream now, not like real sensation. She did not have the words to explain it to herself as a memory and so the experience fell through her fingers like sand. She couldn't hold onto it like an object because she had no name for it.

Death was no longer to be feared, however, she knew that much. It informed her life and gave it meaning and purpose. Life was finite and the presence of death urged her to live. Despite the sadness of Thompson's death, she apprehended her freedom, at that moment, as infinite possibilities. She felt like a yellow wagtail gliding on waves of air, without need for thought or decision, existing only in the sensation of the moment. In killing her father she was free. With Thompson's death they were all free. A fearless Boadicea, ecstatically embracing her life, had finally replaced the surrendered, pitiful Brilliana of earlier in the day.

Listening to Brilliana's words Nathaniel felt only despair. The chaos of death profoundly frightened him, and his

Chapter 18

apprehension was only of meaninglessness at the heart of everything. He wanted control and he needed certainty. He started to count out the night in heartbeats, lost in a silent meditation.

Part Three

'Tis all the heaven we have here below.*

Chapter 19

The sun scorched her eyes open. They had lain away from Thompson's body, but still comforted in the shelter of the spinney. She heard whispering in the gentle early morning breeze, and she craned to look without being seen. A group of men and women were gathered around Thompson. They wore simple, peasant clothes. She brushed the grass from her skirt and walked towards them. 'How are you?' She was confident today as never before.

'We are well. And you kind lady?' A nut-brown, squirrel of a man turned to greet her. Brilliana spoke proudly. 'We are Levellers and we fought in Northampton alongside this brave man lying here, before he fell to the army. We have pamphlets where he wrote about honest and true ideas. He died for freedom rather than live as a slave.'

The group of peasants smiled broadly at Brilliana, as if in one mind. 'We are True Levellers, me lady. We live together on the land, digging our crops in harmony with the natural world, with natural law and with natural rights. The earth is our common treasury. We have taken back the common land that was stolen from the people by the rich and powerful. The Bareshanke was wasteland where we now grow corn. We own nothing and everything. We are equal and just in spirit. We live not far from this place. Would you and your friends care to visit with us and see how we live?'

The men carried Thomson's body to the small piece of common land referred to as the Bareshanke, close to Wellingborrow. At the edge of the trees that lapped at the fields like a green sea, they buried the great strategist of Cromwell's army. They gave him grave goods of his musket and his pamphlet, and allowed the trees and grasses to lend the sea-green colour to his change. William remembered words from the pamphlet, which he spoke with tears filling his eyes, threatening to spill over before collected by his pride. The people of the community rehearsed from the books of Samuel.

During the next week Brilliana, Nathaniel and William rested in the True Leveller community, taking their turns at planting and hoeing. They didn't speak much to each other, but worked hard on the land, each quietly restoring their private faith in humanity. William worked alone, gathering his strength as he gathered wood for the fire. Brilliana thought little of herself, but was immersed in the sensual world around her. She felt the earth pulsate beneath her and the grass and the flowers breathe out in acceptance and understanding. The cobwebs stretched fragile fingers towards dew-dropped leaves, on branches hung heavy with blossom. She played with the little spiders that silently spun down onto her lap. Nathaniel was never alone, but surrounded himself with the True Levellers; he was absorbed in their collective mercy and was able to forget his own fear as he learnt at their feet.

It was a simple peasant life, but co-operative rather than aristocratic. Everything was owned communally and all the food was shared out equally. There were three couples brim-full of sincerity and passion of purpose, with seven ragged, wolf-eyed children between them. A couple of older men who resembled the earth they hoed, spoke little but smiled often, and lived in a temporary structure made from tree branch and leaves. Brilliana was full of wonder at this brave new world, with such courageous people in it.

A red-haired woman, played at the outskirts of the camp. She whispered soft words to the crops from morning to night, but never spoke a word to any of her companions. She sometimes experienced trembling ecstatic visions and would babble about emanations of the Divine, of Ariel the Angel. Her eyes would roll in her head and she would start to dance, kicking legs and arms and spinning like a wild child's top. These manic dance episodes could last for twelve hours before she would drop broken and exhausted onto the earth. Everyone in the community kept a respectful distance from her, whilst ensuring she was fed and clothed and tending to her medicines. She was not of the same world as they, but inhabited the same space.

At the end of that week Brilliana found William staring towards the horizon in a similar clairvoyant trance. He had worked hard on the land, but he was frustrated by the simplicity and routine of life in the community. He would sit still in the twilight hour intent on watching every last glimmer of sunlight. Thompson had illuminated truths for him, and he was not going to turn the light off, he was not yet ready to sleep. 'I need adventure Brilliana. I want to spread the Leveller word. I have heard of the New World and I mean to go there and make it true and honest in Thompson's name.'

Brilliana surrendered in disappointment when she heard these words. She understood that this, unlike when he had first left home, was not an invitation to go with him. He had grown tall and confident with experience. She loved him and she loved this part of him, the part of him that hid from her; that escaped her, the part that she could never catch, not as a child and not now. She smiled and hugged him tightly to her pretending for a moment that she had captured him entirely and was holding him like an anchor. He wrestled free and kissed her lightly on the forehead.

The next day William said goodbye. Brilliana cried gently and felt each tear burrow into and perforate her soul. She had never lived without her brother. He had lacked interest in her at times, he could be cold, but he had always allowed her to accompany him in his adventures, and had never resisted her. They had been conspirators against

CHAPTER 19

their parents as children, and she would miss his safe guidance.

William shook Nathaniel's chafed and calloused hand. They had become friends, a friendship formed through common experience though always paddling in the superficial. Nathaniel reassured himself that William was a Leveller in heart, and he remembered his haloed face at the battle with nail-biting envy. He had no desire to continue on the adventure with William. William, in turn, had seen Nathaniel's fear in battle as clearly as he had seen the death lying at his feet, and when he looked at Nathaniel now he could still see that white mask. William's absence would release Nathaniel from that pitiful gaze and the judgement of the other. Nathaniel would find his freedom.

William felt the excitement tingle deep in his stomach as he jumped effortlessly up onto the back of Thompson's horse. He left the old grey mare for the community, who were grateful. His gnawing desperation to leave meant merciful speed in farewell; for better a sharp pain than a long drawn agony. William kicked the Leveller horse towards the west, as if to chase the sunset forever.

Chapter 20

The summer was a blessed relief for anyone working the land after the cold and wet winter. The ground was heavy and sodden, but the corn the True Levellers planted fairly late in the year flourished on the common ground. Nathaniel and Brilliana had married. Cromwell had made this easy to do, and Brilliana wore no ring as none was needed. Together they had built a shelter from scavenged finds in the countryside around, and it was small and cosy. They had both discovered an inner confidence, which they mined like precious golden nuggets from their experiences. Brilliana was released from servitude by the death of her father. Nathaniel found confidence in simply surviving, but digging the earth also replenished their souls. This confidence decorated their bodies like silks and jewels and they became attractive to each other once more.

Chapter 20

Brilliana had forgiven Nathaniel his thoughtlessness at the sound of battle. She could not forget, but she was able to forgive. He had charmed her with a profound compassion learned from the battle, which had developed a quiet sensitivity to his character. One early afternoon he found a tiny brown rabbit quivering in the field. Its long ears twitched in fear, frighteningly separated from its family. Nathaniel caressed it in his hands, whispering soft, sweet soothing words, and had brought it back to their shelter where he had loved it until it grew strong enough to bound off. He did not try to keep it for his own, as so many would do, and Brilliana loved him for it.

They explored each other and delighted equally in their differences and similarities. She gave him language, revealing her mind to him, as bright as the evening star. She hid her fears and her vulnerabilities from him and she hid her growing dependency on him. He taught her about love, and about men, and the joy and the sorrow they can't help but carry like gifts for women. He kept her safe and cared for her, along with the little rabbit. He did not question their relationship, but was content that they were both alive. He loved her in the simple, practical way that men often do.

Brilliana enjoyed the long evenings sat around the fire, singing songs, laughing and arguing about politics. The community had meetings every week, where they discussed the jobs to be done, and voted on actions. They talked about how much food was left, and how much money, and discussed division of labour and food distribution. They did not have much but they shared what they had. Everyone had a voice and a vote except the children. One of the older boys, named Endurance, questioned why he wasn't allowed to have a vote. The community discussed the age of maturity for weeks before deciding that it should be fourteen, which was largely arbitrary, and based only on physical strength and ability to work.

They called themselves True Levellers, and all agreed that Cromwell had betrayed the revolution. The Civil War had been a fraud. However the Levellers, like Thompson, thought that if all men had the vote Parliament would become more and more radical, as it was the rich that were conservative and maintained the status quo. True Levellers disagreed and demanded economic equality and directed people to take the land back as collective property. Winstanley spoke for this group when he said that God gave the Earth to all people. He blamed the Normans for stealing land and enclosing it for themselves. This private acquisition had led to vast inequality that was unjust and ungodly. It had not only led to starvation and hunger but also to slavery, with a dependency on selling labour for a wage, leaving those who had been masters of their own destiny in the clutches of Lords of Manors and Lords of the Land.

"The earth was not made purposely for you, to be Lords of it, and we to be your Slaves, Servants, and Beggars; but it was made to be a common Livelihood to all, without respect of persons: And that your buying and selling of Land, and the Fruits of it, one to another, is The Cursed thing, and was brought in by War; which hath, and still

CHAPTER 20

does establish murder, and theft, in the branches of some parts of Mankinde over others."*

Brilliana intuitively agreed with the True Levellers. Nathaniel had changed his view from the one he had expressed when walking in the town. He had discovered a deep connection with nature, and a surprising contentment from working the land. He enjoyed the solidarity of all working together for a common purpose and it motivated him to work harder than if he had just been working for himself. Nathaniel had changed. Indeed, he was flourishing in the community. He felt he had found his place in the world. He toiled hard in the fields, and was valued for that, but his understanding of number and money was more invaluable as the True Levellers still needed to trade for vital provisions. He was deeply respected and he held his head high for the first time in his life. Life was predictable and there was certainty in comradeship and tilling the soil. Solidarity provided security.

The community had achieved a respectful view of women as equals; and they easily influenced Nathaniel. He no longer viewed women with the brutal disregard he had earlier. Brilliana had astonished him with her wit, and he had also unearthed admiration for her, and the other women, in the fields where they had tilled the soil at his side. He granted her temporary sovereignty within their utopia, and they both gladly settled for a complacent ceasefire.

Chapter 21

With the death of Thompson and the imprisonment of the other Levellers, Cromwell's black boot of tyranny was stamping out any opposition. Winstanley wrote his pamphlet; 'A Declaration for The Poor and Oppressed People of England', but its circulation led to the demise of the True Leveller community on St George's Hill. The Christian soldiers slayed the dragon slumbering quietly, curled up inside the hill, and piously rejoiced by riding to Ireland to brutally enslave the population. The Rump Parliament began in 1649 and Cromwell declared himself Lord Protector in 1653.

Thomas Hobbes, the English philosopher, wrote Leviathan, safely hidden in continental Europe, and although he was instinctively a royalist, its publication in 1651 justified Cromwell's tyranny. The social contract that citizens had made with the rulers allowed a brutal tyranny. The obligation of the ruler was only to protect his citizens from criminals, and murderers and from invasion. Hobbes argued that the strongest ruler was the best ruler because he could fulfil these obligations most effectively. The duty of the citizen was to obey the ruler in return for his protection. Without a strong leader, according to Hobbes, life would be 'nasty, brutish and short'. This grimy view of human nature, which justified such barbaric tyranny, chimed with Puritan original sin.

Paranoia and fear stank the air of England in 1649. People were poor, hungry and exhausted after the Civil War. The King was dead and most, like Hobbes, were fearful of anarchy. Puritanism was most popular amongst the artisans and shopkeepers: the lower middle-class who could read the Bible, people who were ushering in capitalism. The aristocrats had to move over for the new capitalist classes, who demanded political voice as well as economic power. This earthquake was difficult to control, however, allowing dangerous radicalism to bubble up. It took a leviathan like Cromwell to quell that danger.

After the revolution had been strangled, John Locke was able to describe a gentler social contract later in the century, in his Two Treatises of Government. It premised a less paranoid view of human nature where reason and tolerance were prominent. Nevertheless he shared with Hobbes the idea that people were selfish and he determined that people had natural rights to life, liberty and property. The greengrocers of the time rejoiced in the free-market capitalism that it heralded, and the political rights it espoused.

The radical ideas voiced by True Levellers and other groups of the time gave voice to the poor and dispossessed, living under a veil of ignorance. To Brilliana, communal property made rational sense when she might have nothing. She had nothing to guard from the Hobbesian criminals prowling the country. It was also morally right in a world where some had more than enough, and others were starving. For Brilliana, property ownership was to view the world in the wrong way: whether objects, the environment, animals or people. Ownership physically repelled and nauseated her as it revealed man as tyrant: prowling just under the surface was the insidious desire to control, rule and possess. It was not inevitable, she thought, just wrong, and her life became a struggle against tyranny in all forms. This struggle was instinctive to her and was connected to her profound connection to the natural world, a world of change and flux. She understood that to accept change was to embrace life, and that tyranny stood in opposition to that, it made things dead and still.

As the birds sang the sun-salutation, the community at Bareshanke were discovering Hobbesian dilemmas for themselves. The machinery and handcarts were discovered damaged in the freshness of misty sunrise. Wheels were broken and skewered, tools were snapped and burnt. The crops were trampled in the fields. Most of the destruction was repairable, but some was not. The local town had declared the True Levellers as enemies, on Cromwell's orders. Paranoia shuffled through the men and women like a tethered criminal, eyes glued to the ground in shame.

CHAPTER 21

They did not know how to respond to the threat. Brilliana urged that they go to the town to talk to the people, but the men shook their heads and smirked at the naïveté. Others wanted quiet meditation and prayer to serve as protection because ecstatic trance had revealed that original sin and lack of Godliness was to blame. A few of the men wanted retribution, but the majority finally decided, after blood-hot meetings, that a system of guardianship was needed. It was not the leviathan, but it was a democratic reflection of might is right, and did cause the community some internal problems.

What right did they have to their tools and why did they describe them as their own tools? The discussion centred on the idea that God had given the Earth to man to grow food. Damaging farm tools was ungodly. Thus protection of tools was not protection of property; rather it was protection and honour of God's word, which could not be disputed.

Furthermore, it was argued that protection of communal property from an individual's desire was a good because an individual was thieving from the community, which was bad. This was unlike protection of private property, which was theft from the wider community by the individual, and definitely not a good. The community was an intrinsic good. This argument nearly floundered when someone raised the point that the townsfolk doing the damage were, possibly, in the majority. It was maintained, that protection of communal property was different from protecting private property, however, whoever was attempting to thieve it. Their community was doing God's work and communal property had a special status.

Brilliana felt the hatred of the townsfolk as a tyranny. A violence perpetrated to make her conform and a hatred of difference. Each broken spoke frightened and cowered her. She was reminded of each brutal beating at the hands of her father; each purpled-plum mark had bruised her pride. She had flinched in his face at this corrosion of her identity, as her courage decayed. The rest of the community shared this visceral fear, unsure whether to flee or to fight.

Chapter 22

William arrived wearily saddle-sore at the docks in Bristol where a crowded menagerie of animals and people cluttered the ground. The tall sails of the ships flicked hard in the wind, the ships groaning from their moorings, eager to set sail. He needed a ship for the New World and had been told that he would be able to work his passage.

Buried deep in the crowd was a familiar face with startled hair. Elber Choke was readying some black African slaves for departure, along with some indentured Irish men on some trumped up charges. He unbound their legs and feet so they could board, just leaving their wrists bound. The pennies clattered together in his pockets and he licked his thin lips. The shuffling mass in front of him stared in humiliation at their crabbed feet, as they shambled up the creaking plank into the bowl of the ship. Choke counted them on board by beating each one, and when the last one tipped over the edge, he lost himself in the murk surrounding him.

He had left Northampton a few days ago with the stolen beer and the familiar perpetual smirk playing around his lips. Fearful of Cromwell's army and the Leveller skirmishes he had looped over the top of Oxfordshire before heading round and down to Bristol. His needle-thin, brittle-tempered employer was expecting him at the dock to sort the slaves for passage, and he dared not be late. Choke cursed at the loss of his property and felt the beer to be poor compensation, as he charged through the English countryside.

He had arrived late on the dock yesterday; the gloom was illuminated only by curses and shouts. He had first bustled into the inn to sell his wares, where the rough darkness promised him some recompense. The landlady bought the beer for the soldiers in the backroom. That night Choke landed in a dead weight on the bar floor after cleaning out the local cider supplies. He slept until the drooling morning tugged him over to his employers offices to collect the 'cargo' for departure.

William swerved around the livestock and followed the breeze to the tallest ship in the harbour. He saw a dignified man in plush golden braid; his boots shining like metal, and William decided that he must be in charge of the cream-tiered vision. 'Are you sailing to the New World?' William asked cautiously. The man swept William up in his charms and agreed that he could work his passage, secretly thankful for another hand on deck, with death a probable outcome for many on the journey.

Chapter 22

William scraped his hat deferentially onto the floor, before slowly climbing the gangplank. Half the way up the grey-grained plank whilst treading carefully and purposefully over the struts, something compelled William to turn around. He saw the rat-faced Choke squirming obsequiously by a garishly painted lady, who looked angry. He remembered the tale Brilliana had told of their kidnap and without inhibited thought shouted, 'That man there, Choke, is a dirty robber and a kidnapper and you should fear him, for he will rob and kill you. He kidnapped my sister.'

His voice got lost in the jeer that rose from the crowd as they swarmed around Choke. He was the type of man that Hobbes feared most, the man he was to warn them of and the man he reasoned Cromwell was needed for. Hobbes was not alone in those fears as they were shared by most of the population. They pushed at each other, men pushing men, men pushing women. Choke was a small man and was pulled along by the terrifying mob; he skin-slipped and nearly fell under trampling, tyrannous feet, but dragged himself right. The tyranny of the majority, of the mob, is more frightening than a single tyrant on his horse. Like a shipwrecked boat lost on a rough sea, he bobbed along until shored up by the curiosity of humanity. The huddled masses were naturally intrigued by William's mad ranting on the gangplank of the ship, and the terror of the imagined evil before them.

They pressed to catch a glimpse of him and each press pushed him towards the edge of the dock. Abrupt and shocking came the rough magic of the army, saving him from an unfathomable wet grave, they grabbed his legs and arms, and hoisted him like a dead man out of the crowd. The crowd looked around in astonishment, like cats having lost their mouse. Where had he gone? Had he run away? Had he kidnapped someone? Within thirty seconds the question changed to whether he had ever been there? Like true Cartesians, they easily doubted his existence and looked up towards the ranter on the gangplank, irritated at his deception.

The African and Irish men who had just boarded the ship watched the commotion in quiet dignified silence. Seeing their jailor being carted off they shuffled back down the gangplank and away into the crowds, as fast as their tired, hurt legs could carry them. William felt delighted as he watched them disappear in the confusion, their wrist rope bindings trailing behind them like kites waiting to be cut free. The African slaves had no rights and had nothing to lose by their flight. Maybe they could find work? It was a risk worth taking. The Irish men had contracts and would be free from indenture in five years. Nonetheless the conditions and treatment they had experienced so far felt unsurvivable, and so they ran too.

The soldiers threw Choke onto the cold bone floor of the Church, his hair clinging limply to his head, as if in surrender. The man of God, bustling like a crow, informed the bleary Choke that he was now under the rule of the Ecclesiastical Court, and was to answer to morality crimes. This court had started in the Catholic Cathedral under Charles, but the Puritan clergy had absorbed it as their own, like most of Charles's tyrannies. The landlady of the

CHAPTER 22

inn sniffed into her lace femininity and stuttered that she had looked through a crack in the wall of the inn and had seen Choke 'Laying upon a girl called Patience Green.' She looked as if she were about to faint with the horror. The man of God shook a slow minded head and called for Choke to wear a white shirt in front of tomorrow's congregation and confess his sins.

'Wait!' Sniffed the landlady, 'More than that, this man is a Royalist. He sold us poisoned beer, knowing that Cromwell's loyal soldiers would be resting with us at the inn. All night they were racked with pain and torment as if from the Devil himself. Lucky that they are so strong in constitution, they could not die.' She looked coyly up at one of the soldiers.

A soldier, his strength wrapped in Venice red, his face shadowed with pockmarks, growled. 'We thought we had lost this traitor, until the man on the ship identified him to the crowd. He turned threateningly towards Choke. 'We should have let the crowd kill you. You should have the death penalty'. He paused and turned. 'Shall I take him to the prison?' The man charged with looking after the cities' morality nodded solemnly, agreeing that he should be taken to the prison to await his death. He scribbled a note explaining the charge against Choke. Choke's pleas echoed in the hollow church, like all petty unanswered prayers, as he was dragged away.

William was unaware of any of these events as he settled into his cabin for the journey. He had seen Choke drown in the mob and had smiled with satisfaction. As he lay on his rough sackcloth bunk he smelt the sea-weeded perfume and tasted the salted waves on his skin. It was exotic in its promise and excused his coarse surroundings. The sea-green ocean was coloured by fortunes' gaze for William, and he felt like Odysseus, favoured by the Gods for adventure.

Chapter 23

Three months after Nathaniel and Brilliana had settled, there was an influx of brittle-boned, hungry poor. The crops had failed because of the heavy rains through the winter, and so wheat prices were high. People had less use of common land since the early enclosures, and so were dependent on buying food. The male population had been decimated by the Civil War and many women and children were starving. Some of these women found their way to the community. The community were deeply suspicious at first after the recent local campaign against them, but their innate compassion eventually motivated something of a welcome for the newcomers. The numbers of the Bareshanke swelled like the heads of the corn ripening in the fields.

There were more hands to help with the harvest in the fields, but many more mouths to feed, and the community were unprepared. The children tried to help but mostly bounded like twitching rabbits around the fields in nervous excitement. People worked for longer hours, with little to show for their efforts, and lay exhausted by evening. They still gathered by the fires, but the fires were mealy-mouthed and the logs spat out mean morsels of warmth because they were stunted by the lack of care. Fires are living creatures that need nurture and nourishment to flourish and they will grow cold and resentful if ignored. Religious psalms were sung instead of the old folk tunes as the Puritan spirit of seriousness seeped in, as if through the black earth itself. The first naïve excitement and joy in their righteous community was replaced by a gritted-teeth piety; they were certain they were doing God's work. Idle time became a time of gossip rather than dreaming, and ill winds blew through the camp. The camp became chaotic and ineffective, muddy and damp.

Brilliana, who did not have a serious heart, had no idea or care about what God wanted. She loved the fields of golden corn like fields of yellow wagtails, jittery in the wind, twitching like the children. For her this was beauty made bountiful and it was irreconcilable with the dour, austere gloom that sometimes hung stagnant around the camp. The ears of corn, often gilded by sunlight, were covered in golden threads; fragile and lighter than air, they looked like they would fly off with the tea-orange butterflies that danced around them. She would often sit with the children and make elaborate corn-dollies, weaving the corn solid like the carved wooden sculptures of deities made in Asia. She decorated her home and the other homes with these corn mothers, made prematurely before the last harvest;

Chapter 23

a tradition easily discarded in favour of the delight they brought to the children. They made her hopeful for the harvest and for their future.

The newcomers sheltered, as best they could, from the strange emotional mix of hope and fear that washed like tides through the community. Paranoia stalked at the beaches of their lives, fearing the outsiders who could threaten their dream. Brilliana and Nathaniel were established in the community along with the men, women and children regarded as the original settlers of this island utopia. The newcomers felt unsettled, sometimes hearing paranoia and resentment as strange noises whistling through the trees, like demonic songs sung for them alone. They covered their ears at the sounds and prayed for acceptance. Their arrival had heralded the end of a golden time for the community and they needed to present a gift to ward off the evil spirits, a sacrifice, which could also serve to make themselves necessary.

The rain pattered politely on the sandstone as the True Levellers met for their Friday meeting. One of the newcomers, a tall, greasy woman with bulging bluebottle eyes, raised a shaking, stick like arm towards the end of the meeting, and stuttered. 'I have seen that at times we are not efficient in our work. Today I worked for three hours tending the livestock, but whilst I surrendered to my labour in godly work for our community, I saw others standing and gossiping, idle and wasting. Yet those friends sit and eat the same food.' She bit her lip, not sure of how her gift would be received. 'We are hungry but sometimes people stand idle and that can't be God's will?' Looking around for agreement, she saw unease, and softened her message into one of concern for all the people and community, 'It is true that we don't always know what to do, especially us newcomers. We need help and guidance. It is also true that we need to produce more to stave off the hunger, so that our brave community can survive. I thought I could offer my services to help plan our work, guiding people to where they should be and when. In the name of fairness, and the commune of God of course. Do you agree?' The disheveled group of souls muttered at the innocuousness of the suggestion and people nodded in banal agreement.

The idea was successful and the newcomers found acceptance as the evil spirits retreated. Idleness was formally banished, and the community worked in an ordered way for the first time, which produced more wealth. The godly spirit of seriousness reached fruition and was rewarded in a beauteous bounty of the land. She had gifted order to them and they had sacrificed their free time. Brilliana was certain that the order in itself would have been more than enough as an offering to scare away the demons. She was unsure of the need to lose their free time as well. Several weeks later the same woman sat nearer the fire but her shaking arm was still and strong, muscled by the respect and acceptance of the original settlers. Nathaniel often spent the evenings discussing the economic realities of the community with her, trying to solve the problems with their keen, logical minds. They emptied out of these meetings with grim faces, unwilling to discuss the details.

Chapter 23

All of the friends in the community habitually jostled for favour every evening, as she planned the work schedule of the next day. They would start arriving after the evening dinner and would whisper and joke with her, each in turn engaging in absent-minded flattery. She preened herself in this reflected glory, seeing her image mirrored before her eyes in their fantasies, as a saviour of the True Levellers. The community no longer had time to think, to dream and to create, and they had forgotten that they had ever had that time; memories lay opaque in their relentless toil. They surrendered their time to her authority, which turned easily to tyranny; she had made herself necessary to them. They had failed to realise, without the time to reflect, that she had killed a precious freedom like a kestrel would kill a mouse, and she was laughing as she played with the dead corpse.

Chapter 24

Brilliana held a sanctified place as one of the original settlers, and she had worked hard for the community. Nevertheless, she was alert in the meetings to betrayals of the Leveller spirit as she was loyal to ideas, not the community. She felt uneasy at the air of grim seriousness that hung in the nights now, but she was unsure about how to change that spirit, or whether she ought to change it. If she imposed her will on the community, it would be to surrender to her own tyrant within. She had objected to the loss of free time, but had lost the argument in the face of success and full stomachs. Nathaniel was certain that the seriousness, the planning, the long hours of work, were necessary for their survival. The fires were tended now.

Brilliana had discovered her existence to be as light as a feather since the death of her father. She floated on the high winds, away from the low currents that threatened to

Chapter 24

ground her. She was happy to allow Nathaniel to wade through his serious sensibilities, and easily submitted to his superior knowledge on the subject of survival. She sat by the door and at the edge of things, ready to run if necessary. She thought often of William and his haloed journey. She longed to see him again and this desire was getting harder to resist. She knew that one day she would hear the song of the siren calling her away, and it would be irresistible to her in the freedom of her life.

Despite these intuitions, she did not avoid all responsibility for the present, and she was still hopeful of the ideal. She warned Nathaniel in private, that scarcity was often used as an excuse to justify tyranny and domination. Decisions on organisation could be made co-operatively together, and free time was restorative and therefore led to happier and more productive work. Kill the tyrant and there would be enough to share, and the fires would still keep them warm. Their fear of the outside world had cultivated a rich soil for social tyranny, and she shared in that guilt.

Despite their losses, the community remained courageous; working together co-operatively they ploughed a brand new furrow for human relationships. They thought their survival was important for history, for humanity and for God. Property was still owned communally and political freedoms were shared equally. There were status anxieties within the group and these were the fractures where infection could develop if they didn't take care, if they were not vigilant. Like Gonzalo before them, they should not forget their beginning, thought Brilliana.

Watching Nathaniel in the flickering firelight gave him an unearthly quality, as if he inhabited a dream. Her fingers fiddled as she wove the strands of corn together. The men and women had gathered around him, as they usually did, and they listened intently with a deferential air. He held court and Brilliana thought he looked like a king. She breathed heavily, puffing on her clay pipe, and stared into the fire, looked for dragons and witches dancing in the flicker, or a clairvoyant reflection instead.

The white-boned clay pipe had been the subject of a disagreement between Nathaniel and her earlier that day. She enjoyed evenings by the fire, smoking her pipe and sharing laughter and song. Nathaniel thought smoking and singing were frivolous pastimes when faced with the starvation and oppression rife in their land. His faith was expressed in silence, like his mother, and he shared his private thought with her that singing and smoking were also ungodly. Brilliana exploded at him that, 'She did not realise that he was suddenly speaking for God Himself' and pretended to bow before him. Nathaniel had stormed out of their little house, snapping her pipe in two, before sweeping the scythe through the corn like Death himself, cutting more corn than ten men could. He had learned language from her, and his profit from that was that he had learned how to curse.

She had a spare pipe hidden away and retrieved it from its nest, before spending the rest of that day in idle rebellion. This was only a contrived attitude. She was not honest with Nathaniel about her vulnerability and so his words and actions hurt her more deeply than he could understand. When Nathaniel returned home he probed for guilt but found none. She removed herself from him so the pain would be less. Martyring himself, he tended to the cooking and the cleaning, built the communal fire and now sat holding court, his piousness gleaming like a bejeweled crown on his head.

The True Levellers believed in equality and when Winstanley referred to mankind he included women in that term, unlike most others of this day. Brilliana had felt freedom in the community more keenly than anywhere else. She tilled the soil with the men, cooked with the men and sang with the men. The earth was all of theirs, she owned it as they did, and when she spoke at the meetings with them she was astonished that they listened to her.

Yet still Nathaniel held court like a king and each day was a battle against his rule over her. She could feel the tyrant under his skin. Each day repeated the sensation of running desperately up the pebble beach away from the white water river, fearful of drowning. She spent time too much time constructing rafts to save herself during their time together, and too little time enjoying the water.

Brilliana, however, was unable to hold onto any feeling for long, which came from only paddling in shallow water. This quality was another fortune and allowed her to easily forgive. As soon as she had winced at the angry insight of her personal war with him, she was able to smile secretly at her forgetful love. She shyly remembered the whimsical nights catching rides on the stars above them whilst synchronising their breath with the earth beneath them, then lying helplessly in the fields of golden wagtails. Brilliana sighed, as she missed the laughter they shared, the softness and the sweet, sugary songs. She knew that their song was not over quite yet, that they had a couple more verses to sing before the end of times. Somewhere in the gloom a lone fiddle jigged and Brilliana felt the chaos within, like a shooting star exploding, bringing love and life, transmuting base metal into gold.

Epilogue

Let us then suppose the mind to be, as we say, white paper, void of all characters, without any ideas; how comes it to be furnished? ... To this I answer in one word, from experience.*

This story took place twenty years ago. I could not stay with Nathaniel and the community after the harvest, as my corn deities did not ward of the evil sprits of oppression. I walked through long-leaching night to London town and there, suffered many an adventure, until I met with Margaret Cavendish, a writer. She saw the philosopher in me, and believed that I was someone to help her next great project. Margaret means pearl and both the Margaret's I have known in this life have been pearls; their beauty created through dirt and suffering in nature's glorious alchemy. Margaret Cavendish taught me to read and write, for which I owe her my sensitivity, but she was a Royalist, and there are some things that can't be forgiven.

In this story Cromwell is a fascist: a tyrant, believing himself existentially necessary and chosen by God. Liberalism and communism are ideas that float high on the wind, but are twisted in minds infected by religion. Challenging the idea of tyranny demands that we apprehend the world differently. Tyrants view the world and everything in it as theirs and pursue actions to conquer, control and subordinate. To rid us of the tyrant means to apprehend the world and everything in it in an aesthetic and a creative way. The environment, animals, people are not objects to be owned, but are dynamic changing entities, which we must relate to creatively rather than possessively.

Empiricists have learned to doubt the existence of an eternal self and so our apprehension of self must also be creative. I have tried to be accurate about the person I was, for I am not that person still. There is no eternal self, tyrannical in its constancy. There is no self that is necessary to human kind and to history, and there is no fate. Experience is a creative process and we choose our variable perspectives on it, and in so doing we choose ourselves as temporary.

Only change is certain, a paradox that challenges and calls the tyrant into being, a truth that demands our vigilance. 1649 was a year of tempest, and sea change, and this naturally summoned the tyrant in all of us; the tyrant motivated by fear, motivated to possess the world and self, and to make the turbulent water still and stagnant.

Notes

Prologue

Rene Descartes (1637) Discourse on the Method of Rightly Conducting One's Reason and of Seeking Truth in the Sciences.

Part One

Francis Bacon (1605) The Advancement of Learning.

Chapter One

The Rump Parliament (1649) Act abolishing the kingship.

Chapter Seven

John Milton (1667, 1674) Paradise Lost.

Cornet William Thompson (1649) For A New Parliament by the Agreement of the People: England's Standard Advanced.

Part Two

William Shakespeare (1611) The Tempest.

Chapter Nine

Anon. (1649) To the supream authority of England the Commons assembled in Parliament. The humble petition of diverse wel-affected weomen : of the cities of London and Westminster, the borrough of Southwark, hamblets, and places adjacent. Affecters and approvers of the petition of Sept. 11. 1648.

Chapter Eighteen

Thomas Rainsborough (1647) Putney Debates.

Part Three

Katherine Philips (circa. 1649) Friendship.

Chapter Twenty

Gerrard Winstanley (1649) A Declaration from the Poor Oppressed People of England.

Epilogue

John Locke (1768) An Essay Concerning Human Understanding.

Appendix 1

For a New Parliament by the Agreement of the People: England's Standard Advanced.

A Declaration from M. Will. Thompson and the oppressed People of this nation, now under his conduct in Oxfordshire, Dated at their Randezvouz, May 6. 1649.

Whereas it is notorious to the whole world, that neither the Faith of the Parliament, nor yet the Faith of the Army (formerly made to the People of this nation, in behalf of their Common Right, Freedom and safety) hath bin all observed, or made good, but both absolutely declined and broken, and the People only served with bare words and faire promising Papers, and left utterly destitute of all help or delivery : And that this hath principally bin by the prevalency and treachery of some prominent persons (now domineering over the People) is most evident. The Solemn Engagement of the Army at New-Market and Triploe Heaths by them destroyed, the Councel of Agitators dissolved, the blood of War shed in time of Peace, Petitioners for Common Freedom suppressed by force of armes, and Petitioners abused and terrified, the lawful Tryal by twelve sworn men of the Neighbour-hood subverted and denyed, bloody and tyrannical Courts (called an high Court of justice, and the Councel of State) erected, the power of the sword advanced and set in the Seat of the Magistrates, the Civil Lawes stopt and subverted, and the Military introduced, even to the hostile seizure, imprisonment, tryal, sentence and execution of death, upon divers of the Free People of this Nation, leaving no visible Authority devolving all into a factious Juncto and Councel of State, usurping and assuming the name, stampe and Authority of Parliament, to oppresse, torment and vex the People, whereby all the lives, liberties, and estates, are all subdued to the Wills of those men, no Law, no justice, no right or Freedom, no ease of grievances, no removal of unjust barbarous taxes. no regard to the cryes and groanes of the poore to be had while utter beggary and famin (like a mighty torrent) hath broke in upon us, and already seized upon several parts of the Nation.

Wherefore through an inavoydable necessity, no other means left under heaven, we are inforced to betake our selves to the Law of nature, to defend and preserve our selves and Native Rights, and therefore are resolved as one man (even to the hazard and expence of our lives and

APPENDIX 1

fortunes) to to endeavour the redemption of the Magistracy of England, from under the force of the Sword, to vindicate the Petition of Right, to set the unjustly imprisoned free, to relieve the poore, and settle this Common-wealth upon the grounds of Common Right, Freedom, and Safety.

Be it therefore known to all the free People of England, and to the whole world, that, (chusing rather to die for Freedom than to live as slaves) we are gathered and associated together upon the bare account of Englishmen, with our Swords in our hands, to redeem our selve and the Land of our Nativity, from slavery and oppression, to avenge the blood of War shed in the time of Peace, to have justice for the blood of M. Arnold shot to death at Ware, and for the blood of M. Robert Lockyer, and divers other who of late martial Law were murthered at London.

And upon this our Engagement in behalf of the Commonwealth, we do solemnly agree and protest, that we will faithfully (laying all self respects aside) endeavor the actual relief and settlement of this distressed Nation.

And that all the world may know particularly what we intend, and wherein we will particularly center and acquiesce for ever, not to recede or exceed the least punctillio, we declare from the integrity of our hearts that by the help and might of God we will endeavor the absolute settlement of this distracted Nation, upon that forme and Method by way of an Agreement of the People, tendered as a Peace-offering by Leiut. Col. John Lilburn, M. Will. Walwyn, M. Thomas Prince, and M. Richard Overton, bearing date May 1. 1649. the which we have annexed to this our Declaration as the Standard of our Engagement, thereby owning every part and particular of the Premisses of the said Agreement, Promising and Resolving, to the utmost hazard of our Lives and Abilities, to persue the speedy and full Accomplishment thereof, and to our power, to protect and defend all such as shall Assent or Adhere thereunto : And particularly, for the Preservation and Deliverance of Lieutenant Colonel John Lilburn, M. William Walwyn, M. Thomas Prince, M. Richard Overton, Captain Bray, and M. William Sawyer, from their barbarous and illegal Imprisonments : And we Declare, That if a hair of their heads perish in the hands of those Tyrants who restrain them, That if God shall enable us, we will avenge it seventy times seven fold upon the heads of the Tyrants themselves and their Creatures.

And that till such time as by Gods Assistance we have procured to this Nation the Declared purpose of this our Engagement, we will not Divide nor Disband, nor suffer our selves to be Divided nor Disbanded, resolving with soberness and civility to behave our selves to the Country, to wrong nor abuse any man, to protect all to our power from violence and oppression in all places where we come; resolving to stop the Paiment of all Taxes or Sesments whatsoever, as of Excise, Tythes, and the Tax of ninety thousand pounds per Mensem. &c.

And having once obtained a New Representative, according to the said Agreement, upon such Terms and Limitations therein expressed; We shall then freely lay down our Arms, and return to our several Habitations and Callings.

And concerning the Equity, Necessity and Justice of our undertaking, We appeal to the judgement of the oppressed, betwixt their Destroyers and Us; Whether by the Law of God, of Nature, and Nations, it be not equally justifiable in us to Engage for the Safety and Deliverance of this Nation, as it was with the Netherlanders, and other People for theirs, and that upon the same Principles that the Army engaged at New-Market and Triploe Heaths ; Both Parliament and Army declaring, That it is no resistance of Magistracy, to side with just Principles, and Law of Nature and Nations : And that the Souldiery may lawfully hold the hands of that General, who will turn his Cannon against his Army, on purpose to destroy them : The Sea-men the hands of that Pilot, who wilfully runs his Ship upon a Rock. And therefore (the condition of the Common-wealth considered) we cannot see how it can be otherwise esteemed in us. And upon that account we declare, that we do own, and are resolved to Own all such Persons, either of the Army or Countries, that have already, or shall hereafter, rise up and stand for the Liberties of England, according to the said Agreement of the People : And in particular; We do own and avow the late proceedings in Colonel Scroops, Colonel Harrisons, and Major General Skippons Regiments, declared in their Resolutions published in print; as one man. Resolving to live and dy with them, in their and our just and mutual defence.

And we do implore and invite all such as have any sense of the Bonds and Miseries upon the people; any Bowels of Compassion in them, any Piety, Justice, Honour, or Courage in their Brests, any Affections to the Freedoms of

England, any love to his Neighbor or Native Country, to rise up, and come in to help a Distressed Miserable Nation, To break the Bands of Cruelty, Tyrannie, and Oppression, and set the People Free.

In which service, Trusting to the undoubted goodness of a just and righteous Cause, We shall faithfully discharge the utmost of our Endeavors ; Not sparing the venture of all hardships and hazards whatsoever, and leave the Successe to God.

Signed by me William Thompson, at our Randez-

vouz in Oxfordshire, neer Banbury, in behalf of

my Self, and the Rest Engaged with me,

May 6. 1649.

Appendix 2

A declaration from the poor oppressed people of England, directed to all that call themselves, or are called Lords of Manors, through this nation; that have begun to cut, or that through fear and covetousness, do intend to cut down the woods and trees that grow upon the Commons and Waste Land. Printed in the Yeer, 1649.

We whose names are subscribed, do in the name of all the poor oppressed people in England, declare unto you, that call your selves lords of Manors, and Lords of the Land, That in regard the King of Righteousness, our Maker, hath inlightened our hearts so far, as to see, That the earth was not made purposely for you, to be Lords of it, and we to be your Slaves, Servants, and Beggers; but it was made to be a common Livelihood to all, without respect of persons: And that your buying and selling of Land, and the Fruits of it, one to another, is The cursed thing, and was brought in by War; which hath, and still does establish murder, and theft, In the hands of some branches of Mankinde over others, which is the greatest outward burden, and unrighteous power, that the Creation groans under: For the power of inclosing Land, and owning Propriety, was brought into the Creation by your Ancestors by the Sword; which first did murther their fellow Creatures, Men, and after plunder or steal away their Land, and left this Land successively to you, their Children. And therefore, though you did not kill or theeve, yet you hold that cursed thing in your hand, by the power of the Sword; and so you justifie the wicked deeds of your Fathers; and that sin of your Fathers, shall be visited upon the Head of you, and your Children, to the third and fourth Generation, and longer too, till your bloody and theeving power be rooted out of the Land.

And further, in regard the King of Righteousness hath made us sensible of our burthens, and the cryes and groanings of our hearts are come before him: We take it as a testimony of love from him, That our hearts begin to be freed from slavish fear of men, such as you are; and that we find Resolutions in us, grounded upon the inward law of Love, one towards another, To Dig and Plough up the Commons, and waste Lands through England; and that our conversation shall be so unblameable, That your Laws shall not reach to oppress us any longer, unless you by your Laws will shed the innocent blood that runs in our veins.

APPENDIX 2

For though you and your Ancestors got your Propriety by murther and theft, and you keep it by the same power from us, that have an equal right to the Land with you, by the righteous Law of Creation, yet we shall have no occasion of quarrelling (as you do) about that disturbing devil, called Particular propriety: For the Earth, with all her Fruits of Corn, Cattle, and such like, was made to be a common Store-house of Livelihood to all Mankinde, friend, and foe, without exception.

And to prevent your scrupulous Objections, know this, That we Must neither buy nor sell; Money must not any longer (after our work of the Earths community is advanced) be the great god, that hedges in some, and hedges out others; for Money is but part of the Earth: And surely, the Righteous Creator, who is King, did never ordain, That unless some of Mankinde, do bring that Mineral (Silver and Gold) in their hands, to others of their own kinde, that they should neither be fed, nor be clothed; no surely, For this was the project of Tyrant-flesh (which Land-lords are branches of) to set his Image upon Money. And they make this unrighteous Law, That none should buy or sell, eat, or be clothed, or have any comfortable Livelihood among men, unless they did bring his Image stamped upon Gold or Silver in their hands.

And whereas the Scriptures speak, That the mark of the Beast is 666, the number of a man; and that those that do not bring that mark in their hands, or in their foreheads, they should neither buy nor sell, Revel. 13.16. And seeing the numbering Letters round about the English money make 666, which is the number of that Kingly Power and

Glory, (called a Man) And seeing the age of the Creation is now come to the Image of the Beast, or Half day. And seeing 666 is his mark, we expect this to be the last Tyrannical power that shall raign; and that people shall live freely in the enioyment of the Earth, without bringing the mark of the Beast in their hands, or in their promise; and that they shall buy Wine and Milk, without Money, or without price, as Isiah speaks.

For after our work of the Earthly community is advanced, we must make use of Gold and Silver, as we do of other metals, but not to buy and sell withal; for buying and selling is the great cheat, that robs and steals the Earth one from another: It is that which makes some Lords, others Beggers, some Rulers, others to be ruled; and makes great Murderers and Theeves to be imprisoners, and hangers of little ones, or of sincere-hearted men.

And while we are made to labor the Earth together, with one consent and willing minde; and while we are made free, that every one, friend and foe, shall enjoy the benefit of their Creation, that is, To have food and rayment from the Earth, their Mother; and every one subiect to give accompt of his thoughts, words, and actions to none, but to the one onely righteous Judg, and Prince of Peace; the Spirit of Righteousness that dwells, and that is now rising up to rule in every Creature, and in the whole Globe. We say, while we are made to hinder no man of his Priviledges given him in his Creation, equal to one, as to another; what Law then can you make, to take hold upon us, but Laws of Oppression and Tyranny, that shall enslave or spill the blood of the Innocent? And so your Selves, your Judges,

Lawyers, and Justices, shall be found to be the greatest Transgressors, in, and over Mankinde.

But to draw neerer to declare our meaning, what we would have, and what we shall endevor to the uttermost to obtain, as moderate and righteous Reason directs us; seeing we are made to see our Privileages, given us in our Creation, which have hitherto been denied to us, and our Fathers, since the power of the Sword began to rule, And the secrets of the Creation have been locked up under the traditional, Parrat-like speaking, from the Universities, and Colledges for Scolars, And since the power of the murdering, and theeving Sword, formerly, as well as now of late yeers, hath set up a Govenment, and maintains that Government; for what are prisons, and putting others to death, but the power of the Sword to enforce people to that Government which was got by Conquest and Sword, and cannot stand of it self, but by the same murdering power? That Government that is got over people by the Sword and kept by the Sword, is not set up by the King of Righteousness to be his Law, but by Covetousness, the great god of the world; who hath been permitted to raign for a time, times, and dividing of time and his government draws to the period of the last term of his allotted time; and then the Nations shall see the glory of that Government that shall rule in Righteousness, without either Sword or Spear,

And seeing further, the power of Righteousness in our hearts, seeking the livelihood of others as well as our selves, hath drawn forth our bodies to begin to dig, and plough, in the Commons and waste Land, for the reasons already declared,

And seeing and finding ourselves poor, wanting Food to feed upon, while we labor the Earth to cast in seed, and to wait till the first crop comes up; and wanting Ploughs, Carts, Corn, and such materials to plant the Commons withal, we are willing to declare our condition to you, and to all, that have the Treasury of the Earth, locked up in your Bags, Chests, and Barns, and will offer up nothing to this publike Treasury; but will rather see your fellow Creatures starve for want of Bread, that have an equal right to it with your selves, by the Law of Creation: But this by the way we onely declare to you, and to all that follow the subtle art of buying and selling the Earth with her Fruits, meerly to get the Treasury thereof into their hands, to lock it up from them, to whom it belongs; that so, such covetous, proud, unrighteous, selfish flesh, may be left without excuse in the day of Judgment.

And therefore, the main thing we aym at, and for which we declare our Resolutions to go forth, and act, is this, To lay hold upon, and as we stand in need, to cut and fell, and make the best advantage we can of the Woods and Trees, that grow upon the Commons, To be a stock for our selves, and our poor Brethren, through the land of England, to plant the Commons withal; and to provide us bread to eat, till the Fruit of our labors in the Earth bring forth increase; and we shall meddle with none of your Proprieties (but what is called Commonage) till the Spirit in you, make you cast up your Lands and Goods, which were got, and still is kept in your hands by murder, and theft; and then we shall take it from the Spirit, that hath conquered you, and not from our Swords, which is an abominable, and unrighteous power, and a destroyer of the Creation: But the Son of man comes not to destroy, but to save.

And we are moved to send forth this Declaration abroad, to give notice to every one whom it concerns, in regard we hear and see, that some of you, that have been Lords of Manors, do cause the Trees and Woods that grow upon the Commons, which you pretend a Royalty unto, to be cut down and sold, for your own private use, Thereby the Common Land, which your own mouths doe say belongs to the poor, is impoverished, and the poor oppressed people robbed of their Rights, while you give them cheating words, by telling some of our poor oppressed Brethren, That those of us that have begun to Dig and Plough up the Commons, will hinder the poor; and so blinde their eyes, that they see not their Priviledge, while you, and the rich Free-holders make the most profit of the Commons, by your over-stocking of them with Sheep and Cattle; and the poor that have the name to own the Commons, have the least share therein; nay, they are checked by you, if they cut Wood, Heath, Turf, or Furseys, in places about the Common, where you disallow.

Therefore we are resolved to be cheated no longer, nor be held under the slavish fear of you no longer, seing the Earth was made for us, as well as for you. And if the Common Land belongs to us who are the poor oppressed, surely the woods that grow upon the Commons belong to us likewise: therefore we are resolved to try the uttermost in the light of reason, to know whether we shall be free men, or slaves. If we lie still, and let you steale away our Birthrights, we perish; and if we Petition we perish also, though we have paid taxes, given free quarter, and ventured our lives to preserve the Nations freedom as much as you, and therefore by the law of contract with you, freedom in the land is our portion as well as yours, equal with you: And if we strive for freedom, and your murdering, governing Laws destroy us, we can but perish.

Therefore we require, and we resolve to take both Common Land, and Common woods to be a livelihood for us, and look upon you as equal with us, not above us, knowing very well, that England the land of our Nativity, is to be a common Treasury of livelihood to all, without respect of persons.

So then, we declare unto you, that do intend to cut our Common Woods and Trees, that you shall not do it; unlesse it be for a stock for us, as aforesaid, and we to know of it, by a publick declaration abroad, that the poor oppressed, that live thereabouts, may take it, and employ it, for their publike use, therefore take notice we have demanded it in the name of the Commons of England, and of all the Nations of the world, it being the righteous freedom of the Creation.

Likewise we declare to you that have begun to cut down our Common Woods and Trees, and to fell and carry away the same for your private use, that you shall forbear, and go no farther, hoping, that none that are friends to the Commonwealth of England, will endeavour to buy any of those Common Trees and Woods of any of those Lords of Mannors, so called, who have, by the murdering and cheating law of the sword, stoln the Land from younger brothers, who have by the law of Creation, a standing portion in the Land, as well, and equall with others. Therefore we hope all Wood-mongers will disown all such private merchandise, as being a robbing of the poor oppressed, and take notice, that they have been told our resolution: But if any of you that are Wood-mongers, will buy it of the poor, and for their use, to stock the Commons, from such as may be appointed by us to sell it, you shall have it quietly, without diminution; but if you will slight us in this thing, blame us not, if we make stop of the Carts you send and convert the Woods to our own use, as need requires, it being our own, equal with him that calls himself the Lord of the Mannor, and not his peculiar right, shutting us out, but he shall share with us as a fellow-creature.

For we say our purpose is, to take those Common Woods to sell them, now at first, to be a stock for our selves, and our children after us, to plant and manure the Common land withall; for we shall endeavour by our righteous acting not to leave the earth any longer intangled unto our children, by self-seeking proprietors; But to leave it a free store-house, and common treasury to all, without respect of persons; And this we count is our dutie, to endeavour to the uttermost, every man in his place (according to the nationall Covenant which the Parliament set forth) a Reformation to preserve the peoples liberties, one as well as another: As well those as have paid taxes, and given free quarter, as those that have either born the sword, or taken our moneys to dispose of them for publike use: for if the Reformation must be according to the word of God, then every one is to have the benefit and freedom of his creation, without respect of persons; we count this our duty, we say, to endeavour to the uttermost, and so shall leave those that rise up to oppose us without excuse, in their day of Judgment; and our precious blood, we hope, shall not be dear to us, to be willingly laid down at the door of a prison, or foot of a gallows, to justifie this righteous cause; if those that have taken our money from us, and promised to give us freedom for it, should turn Tyrants against us: for we must not fight, but suffer.

And further we intend, that not one, two, or a few men of us shall sell or exchange the said woods, but it shall be known publikly in Print or writing to all, how much every such, and such parcell of wood is sold for, and how it is laid out, either in victualls, corn, ploughs, or other materials necessary.

And we hope we may not doubt (at least we expect) that they that are called the great Councel and powers of England, who so often have declared themselves, by promises and Covenants, and confirmed them by multitude of fasting daies, and devout Protestations, to make England a free people, upon condition they would pay moneys, and adventure their lives against the successor of the Norman Conqueror; under whose oppressing power England was enslaved; And we look upon that freedom promised to be the inheritance of all, without respect of persons; And this cannot be, unless the Land of England be freely set at liberty from proprietors, and become a common Treasury to all her children, as every portion of the Land of Canaan was the Common livelihood of such and such a Tribe, and of every member in that Tribe, without exception, neither hedging in any, nor hedging out.

We say we hope we need not doubt of their sincerity to us herein, and that they will not gainsay our determinate course; howsoever, their actions will prove to the view of all, either their sinceritie, or hypocrisie: We know what we speak is our priviledge, and our cause is righteous, and if they doubt of it, let them but send a childe for us to come before them, and we shall make it manifest four wayes.

First, by the National Covenant, which yet stands in force to bind Parliament and people to be faithful and sincere, before the Lord God Almighty, wherein every one in his several place hath covenanted to preserve and seek the liberty each of other, without respect of persons.

Secondly, by the late Victory over King Charls, we do claime this our pnviledge, to be quietly given us, out of the hands of Tyrant-Government, as our bargain and contract with them; for the Parliament promised, if we would pay taxes, and give free quarter, and adventure our lives against Charls and his party, whom they called the Common enemy, they would make us a free people; These three being all done by us, as well as by themselves, we claim this our bargain, by the law of contract from them, to be a free people with them, and to have an equall priviledge of Common livelihood with them, they being chosen by us, but for a peculiar worke, and for an appointed time, from among us, not to be our oppressing Lords, but servants to succour us. But these two are our weakest proofs. And yet by them (in the light of reason and equity that dwells in mens hearts) we shall with ease cast down, all those former enslaving Norman reiterated laws, in every Kings raigne since the Conquest, which are as thornes in our eyes, and pricks in our sides, and which are called the Ancient Government of England.

Thirdly we shall prove that we have a free right to the land of England, being born therein as well as elder brothers, and that it is our equal right with them, and they with us, to have a comfortable livlihood in the earth, without owning any of our own kinde, to be either Lords, or Land-Lords over us: And this we shall prove by plain Text of Scripture, without exposition upon them, which the Scholars and great ones generally say, is their rule to walk by.

Fourthly, we shall prove it by the Righteous Law of our Creation, That mankinde in all his branches, is the Lord of the Earth and ought not to be in subjection to any of his own kinde without him, but to live in the light of the law of righteousness, and peace established in his heart.

And thus in love we have declared the purpose of our hearts plainly, without flatterie, expecting love, and the same sincerity from you, without grumbling or quarreling, being Creatures of your own Image and mould, intending no other matter herein, but to observe the Law of righteous action, endeavouring to shut out of the Creation, the cursed thing, called Particular Propriety, which is the cause of all wars, bloud-shed, theft, and enslaving Laws, that hold the people under miserie.

Signed for and in behalf of all the poor oppressed people of England,

and the whole world.

About the Author

Caroline Sanders lives in Northampton and has a degree in politics from the University of Warwick and a master's degree in philosophy from the University of Birmingham, alongside therapeutic qualifications. In her career she has taught philosophy, critical thinking and politics, facilitating philosophical enquiries and communities of learning, as well as being involved in community activism. She has also supported and empowered adults, families, children and young people to discover ways to better mental health and connection, and has written on mutual aid solutions to adverse childhood experiences and health inequality.

She is a vegetarian, enjoys nature connection and Zen mindfulness practice. She lives with her partner and two sons, who often state grimly that they believe her to be a witch. Brought up by Marxists, as a child she believed the world was never more than a year away from revolution ... and she still waits.

Printed in Great Britain
by Amazon